THE
MAGICIAN

MAYA DANIELS

BOOKS

Vinci Books

vinci-books.com

Published by Vinci Books Ltd in 2026

1

Copyright © Maya Daniels 2020

The author has asserted their moral right to be identified as the author of this work in accordance with the Copyright, Designs and Patents Act 1988. This work is a work of fiction. Names, characters, places and incidents are the product of the author's imagination or are used fictitiously. Any resemblance to actual persons, living or dead, places and incidents is entirely coincidental.
All rights reserved. No part of this publication may be copied, reproduced, distributed, stored in any retrieval system, or transmitted in any form or by any means, including photocopying, recording, or other electronic or mechanical methods, nor used as a source for any form of machine learning including AI datasets, without the prior written permission of the publisher.
The publisher and the author have made every effort to obtain permissions for any third party material used in this book and to comply with copyright law. Any queries in this respect should be brought to the attention of the publisher and any omissions will be corrected in future editions.
A CIP catalogue record for this book is available from the British Library.
Paperback ISBN: 9781036705824
The EU GPSR authorised representative is Logos Europe, 9 rue Nicolas Poussion, 17000 La Rochelle, France contact@logoseurope.eu

By Maya Daniels

The Necronomicon Guardian
The Magician
The High Priestess

Chronicles of Forbidden Witchery Series
Resting Witch Face
Pitch a Witch
Witch Please
Payback is a Witch

The Broken Halos Series
The Devil is in the Details
Speak of the Devil
Encounter with the Devil
The Devil in Disguise
To Look the Devil in the Eye
Better The Devil You Know
Give a Devil His Due

The Last Note Series
Sound
Sonata

Hidden Portals Trilogy

Venus Trap

The First Secret

Daywalker Series

Investigated

Infiltrated

Instigated

Initiated

Infuriated

Ignited

Infernal Regions for the Unprepared

Black Hand

Lower World

Everlasting Fire

Place of Torment

Hellfire To Come

The Courtless Fae Series

Secret Origins

New Blood Rising

Rebirth - Risorgimento

Overthrown - Rovesciamento

Recognition - Riconoscimento

The Gatekeepers Legacy
Legacy of Water
Legacy of Fire
Legacy of Spirit

Honor Among Thieves
Stolen Magic
Stolen Oath

By Maya Daniels
The Cursed Kingdom

Chapter One

I often wondered what made people such dimwits.

Was it fear of someone being a more decent being than them? Did they see something in that person that rubbed their demons wrong, so they decided it was a good thing to make the life of the poor soul miserable? Were they overcompensating for something? Whatever it might be, it definitely made me see red and get in their face. One could argue that those dimwits rubbed my demons wrong, bringing out ghosts from the past when I was the one bullied. I should stay out of those things, yet I couldn't let it go. I jumped at every chance to put them in their place.

A double-edged sword is what I call it.

Rubbing at my ribs, which were smarting from being pushed into the banister of the stairway with two of the said dimwits looming over me, I nudged Glenda further behind my back. The poor girl was shaking so hard I could hear her teeth chattering like a rattlesnake. Neither her nor the two men blocking our path were people I liked to hang around with, but I'd be damned if I let them push a girl around just because her magic wasn't strong enough to fight them off.

Glenda was a seer, not an offense mage like the two glaring at me.

"You were saying?" Squaring off with Jonas and Astor was not a smart move on my part if I didn't want additional problems but that didn't stop the words spilling from my mouth. These two were the killers with the highest score of eliminated targets in my clan. Because no matter what kind of fancy and sophisticated names they used for us, at the end of the day that's what we were.

Killers.

Knowing I needed to stay out of sight when it comes to these two never stopped me from sticking my nose where it didn't belong, because my mother's words haunted my every breath: "For evil to run amok dear, all that needs to happen is for good people to do nothing."

Not that I considered myself a good person. Not by a long shot.

"You haven't learned your place yet, have you kibitzer?" Jonas, the taller of the two sneered at me, his dark, beady eyes flaring with a manic glint. "You should thank your uncle daily for his protection because that's the only reason you are still breathing." If he expected me to be offended by his snide words, he would be sorely disappointed. I'd been insulted worse in this hornet's nest I called home than their pathetic use of kibitzer also known as a meddler. Vagrant was their second insult of choice.

"That is a great idea!" Clapping my hands excitedly I blinked at him like an idiot. "I'll go right now to express my gratitude." Gasping, I folded both hands like a prayer. "I'll tell him how you reminded me to do it, too. He will be so happy to hear that." A low move on my part but an effective one. I tried not to use my uncle as a crutch but it was inevitable at times.

Jonas jerked back, his head turning left and right to see if anyone was eavesdropping, because someone is always eavesdropping around here. Assured there was no one around, he clenched his jaw, white sparks coming out of his fingers in short bursts. My own magic reared up in response, coiled like a snake ready to strike if he dared attack me.

Glenda whimpered behind me.

"Get out of my face, Jonas, before both of us regret this encounter. Last time this kibitzer got unhinged, the house almost burned down." A shaking hand wrapped around the shirt on my back, a reminder that the woman behind me was just about ready to faint from fear. "Astor, take your friend in the greenhouse out back to calm down. If he knows what's good for him, he will leave Glenda alone."

"Is that a threat, kibitzer?"

Astor snatched Jonas by the arm, holding him back when he took a step forward. His glower promised retribution, and a shiver slithered up my spine. This argument will not be the last thing I deal with when it comes to this particular mage. But, he could get in line. I'd been watching my back from the age of five in this place. The day I stepped foot through the heavy oak doors was the moment I learned if I was going to survive, I'd better grow eyes at the back of my head.

"No, I wouldn't dream of making a threat." His menacing smile appeared much too fast on his unassuming face. "It's a promise. One I'm going to keep."

"I wouldn't add more enemies around here." Astor, the quieter of the duo, frowned at me as if it was my fault we were having this conversation. "You have enough problems as it is."

"You don't say." I deadpanned, my hand itching to slap him for stating the obvious. The entire mage community knew I was undesirable in my own home—the ill-bred shame, who was also a public secret.

"The day will come, kibitzer." Jonas threw the words over his shoulder while Astor tugged him down the long stairway. "And when it does ... I'll be the last face you see before your miserable life ends."

"I can't wait." A genuine smile stretched my lips, and it forced Astor to do a double take, his mouth dropping open. "When it comes it'll mean I don't have to hold back. It means I'll have nothing to lose. I'll see you then." With a wink, I watched the two mages trod down the wooden stairs, their feet silent.

Reaching behind me, I pried Glenda's ice-cold fingers from my shirt. Taking her by the arm, I led her down the hallway to the first place I could think of. The sound of cracking hinges as I opened the door to the attic were like gunshots through the silence. I pushed the still trembling woman ahead of me, following behind her as my own heartbeat thundered in my ears now that the adrenaline had worn off, muting any sound that would alert me of danger. A stupid slip up on my part, but I couldn't help that those two got to me. They'd get under anyone's skin that had an ounce of brains just to stay alive.

You don't get to play with killers and expect to breathe for long.

Glenda crumbled on the floor as soon as we reached the top of the stairs. Lost in my own thoughts, I was too late to react, tripping over the heap at my feet and sprawling on the wooden planks. Half of my body hit the floorboards hard, while the other half tangled with her legs. It look a lot of twisting, groaning, and yelping between the two of us to roll to my back and get free of her limbs, and I laid there for a minute staring at the slanted beams of the roof. She plopped down the same, stretching out next to me with our hands barely touching. The skylight windows were casting sheets of sunlight over the old trunks and boxes littering the attic, the dust motes dancing around us like tiny little fairies.

"Thank you, Ch—"

"You can stop right there." I slapped the back of her hand with mine, cutting her off. "Don't make me out to be some hero, Glenda. I got involved because I love ruining the day of those two mother truckers." Which was a lie. I would want nothing more than to be as far from them as possible.

"You say that every time you help me out." She snorted ungracefully. "You should learn how to accept gratitude if you are to take the bruises meant for me."

"What bruises?" As if reminded of the abuse they received from the banister, my ribs sent a sharp pain through my side and stole my breath. "I didn't feel a thing." My voice was strained, the words pushed out through clenched teeth.

"Right." Glenda's head popped above me when she lifted herself on one elbow. "Of course you didn't."

Her hair escaped the messy bun she had at the back of her head, tendrils of flame red curls framing her still ashen face. I didn't like how her dark forest eyes watched me with knowing. Like everything I was trying to hide, all my secrets, were plain and visible to her. I really should stop getting involved in things like this. Jonas got to her more times than I could stop it, so it wasn't like I helped her much. Plus, I didn't really like her. Actually I didn't know her well enough to know if I liked her. It wasn't like we were friends or something.

Those like me, like us, didn't have friends.

It was a weakness we couldn't afford.

Another rule I broke.

"You should stay here a little longer." Rolling away from her, I jumped on my feet and dusted off my pants. "Those dumbnuts will be in training in about fifteen ... twenty minutes. You should be good to go after that."

"Okay." Tilting her face up to look at me, Glenda stayed stretched out on the floor. "You should work on your cursing meanwhile."

"What?" Frowning at her, I got more confused when she giggled like a child.

"Dumbnuts, and other curse words I've heard you use are not very intimidating." Shaking her head, her pitying gaze sent a jolt through my gut. "If they are even curse words," she mumbled under her breath while I gaped at her.

"That's what you took away from my badassery out there?" Flinging a hand, I stabbed a finger in the direction of the stairs. "You saw them leaving, right?" Glenda nodded her head so fast that her half-unraveled bun bounced off the back of her head like a squirrel on steroids. "I'd say I'm intimidating enough."

"I think it's more the crazed look you get in your eyes." Her mouth clamped shut and she bit the inside of it, staring at me with wide eyes as if she didn't mean for the words to come out. "Sorry."

Her summer dress had ridden up above her knees, and the purple bruise on her thigh, a week old was my guess, froze any retort I had ready. The yellow fabric and her pale skin made the abused flesh stand out stark as if staring at me accusingly. It was a reminder that I might not be helping her at all, only making things worse. I added a reminder to follow her more often to the back of my mind. I had a feeling the two dumbnuts were waiting to corner her when she was alone, and we couldn't have that.

You are not her keeper. A voice reminded me that I should stop middling in things around here. *'you are not even her friend.'*

"Listen …"

Deep, distorted voices floated from the bottom of the stairs pulling my attention to them. I strained my ears to hear if it's the person I was looking to see when I came across Glenda and the two bullies. The conversation was muted by distance and the closed door of the attic, but I'd recognize that deep timbre anywhere. It was the patron of the house, talking to someone that arranged a meeting with him very late last night. Okay, so I snooped, but it wasn't like I had anything better to do since I was on a timeout from training after my last fiasco. Excitement spread through me like a wave of warm air speeding up my heartbeat.

"Stay here a bit longer, then you should be good to go." Ignoring Glenda's confused face, I rushed down the stairs on the tips of my toes.

Silent as a church mouse, I pressed my ear on the cool wooden door and strained to hear anything being said. The voices were indistinguishable, the two men having moved further down the hall by the time I reached the bottom. With one last look to assure myself that Glenda was not following, and to make sure no one was around to hear the God-awful sound of the stupid hinges, I cracked the door open. Wincing, I stuck my head out looking in both directions, and when not a soul stirred, I slinked out of the attic to follow the men.

The main office was the only place the meeting would take place, so I headed in that direction on silent feet.

Knowing I'd get in more trouble than it was worth, never stopped me from doing anything. Glenda was a pure example of my meddling tendencies. Still, I carefully reached the ornate doors, which were sealed shut, and while biting on my lower lip I debated the best position for some major eavesdropping. The window at the end of the long hallway got my attention, so grinning like a fool, I pulled it open and climbed out.

Avoiding looking down while balancing on the tips of my sneakers on the brick ledge, I inched closer to the window of the office. If anyone walked past and glanced up I'd be doomed, but normally at that hour in the morning everyone was busy training or out on a mission, so I should be good.

My fingers ached from clutching the sharp edges of the brick house, but determination did not fail me. When I was lined up with the windowsill, I held my breath but no sound came out of the office. Frowning, I leaned to the side enough to peek through the glass with one eye. Luckily, Master Bowmen was laser focused on the man sitting across from him. Unfortunately for me, that person was sitting with their back toward me so I couldn't see their face. And the second bad thing, which of course I felt a moment too late, was the wards prickling my skin.

Silence wards.

Pulling back, I thumped my head on the bricks, instantly grimacing from the sharp bite the edge gave my forehead. This was useless. With a deep sigh, I looked three stories down at the immaculate lawn and perfectly trimmed rose bushes. Should I jump and possibly break or sprain something? I eyed the long way back to the open window of the hallway. If I hurried, I could get back inside with none the wiser. Mind made up, I clawed my way back, arms and legs shaking from the strain of keeping my body plastered to the outside walls. Pushing the window further open, I lifted my knee to climb back in. The fabric of my stretchy pants caught on the uneven wood, which stabbed my leg in the process.

Pressing my lips tight so I didn't make a sound, I lost my balance and the tip of my sneaker slipped off the tiny ledge. I gripped the sides of the windowsill with a desperation of a drowning man who was grasping at a straw, then dove through the window like a bull through flimsy gates. The loud thump of my body hitting the floor might've been ignored if I kept the squeak to myself. It passed my lips despite my effort to be silent, and a second later the door of the office opened, Master Bowmen's face frowning at me upside down from my position on the floor. His eyes darted from me to the open window twice before he turned a frosty glare at my red, burning face, which curdled my blood.

"I will call for you shortly, Charlie." His clipped, deep voice sounded like an executioner's ax hitting the chopping block. "Get out of here, girl."

He missed my whimper when he slammed the door of the office with a resounding boom.

Chapter Two

Later that afternoon I blinked at Master Bowmen, his stony face betraying nothing, not even an iota of humor indicating that all this was a joke. While my ears were buzzing, my heart thundered like a war drum against my ribs. I subtly wiped my sweaty palms off the stretchy yoga pants I put on that morning as my way of pretending to exercise. The deep lines etched on Master Bowmen's face spread across it like a topographic map, holding my undivided attention. I took a moment to compose myself from the shock of what I'd heard. I knew there was a reason I'd been adamant to eavesdrop on his meeting, and I'd felt it in my bones. Even the breath passing my lips was as loud as a chainsaw in the deathly silence that fell over us, coiling around my neck like a noose.

"I'm sorry, what?"

Yeah, I know. Not the most competent reply when given your first target, but this is neither a common thing, nor an expected one. Targets were given by the hour around here, but not to me.

Never to me.

My name is Charlie Jansen, and I am an assassin mage of the Jansen clan. Meaning we had a flavor of magic, as they called it, and it made us the deadliest people alive. And clan Jansen was at the top of the food chain between the seven clans in existence when it came to eliminated targets and jobs well done. If Master Bowmen was telling the story, he would've made sure to mention that we had an immaculate record because I was never given a task. Apparently, my magic was unpredictable and volatile. Oh, and I was a klutz.

The nerve!

Okay, fine. I tripped over my feet sometimes, but that was because I was lost in thought or daydreaming. Also, a few times I accidently put my trainers in the infirmary, but that was only because I got a little too excited to use my magic since I'd been restrained from touching it for the most part. So really, it wasn't my fault. Master Bowmen was to blame for warding my powers, although he claimed it was for my own good. Little did he know I learned how to unravel the wards by accident, much to my delight. Take that Master Bowmen with your ridiculous excuses of protection.

Right, what a joke. Leave me defenseless in the hornet's nest, why don't you? I thought.

And I did set a fire to our arsenal that one time, but how was I to see the trap wards that were placed around it? Shouldn't they have notified everyone, for safety's sake if nothing else? Survival instinct kicked in when the wards slithered over my skin like vile slugs, and my magic attacked everything in sight, annihilating a depository full of bottled spells, enhancers, and other irreplaceable gadgets that we would keep secret until the day we went to our graves. It was our key advantage over the rest of the clans.

"Was" being the crucial part of that thought.

We didn't have it anymore.

Was that why he resorted to signing up a target for me? Was it a punishment? Master Bowmen's lips twisted into a squiggly line, the grimace similar to the one when he ate half a lemon, swallowing it mostly unchewed in his rush to stop me from talking at the monthly formal dinner all of us have to attend as a mandatory part of being a member of our clan. Unsure if he read my mind about the "accident" or if he was about to shout "Got ya!" because this must be a joke, I stood there gawking at him. If I didn't know better, I'd say he made it his mission to keep me away from everyone, and now this. *Or he is keeping everyone away from you, because you know, you are volatile and all that.* I kicked the stupid voice in my head to silence it.

"The file should be arriving early in the 'morrow." A weary sigh stumbled out of his mouth, his thin shoulders hunching over. "If it was up to me ..."

Here we go. This will be familiar territory, I thought.

"... I would give the mission to someone else." Turning down the hall, he motioned for me to walk with him. "You were specifically requested, alias, so I have no choice but to obey."

Trepidation clawed at my innards as I kept pace with him, my outside calm at war with the turmoil battering my skull. Needing more time before opening that Pandora's box, I decided to change the subject.

"You've been reading those historical novels again, haven't you?" After making sure that no one was within earshot, I tugged harder on my sleeves and pulled them over my knuckles. "You are using words like 'morrow and alias." His chuckle didn't warm me like it usually did.

"There is beauty in the past that the present is lacking."

With a twitchy shrug, he glanced sideways at me, that one wary flick of his eyes snapping my spine ramrod straight. "I don't like this, nibbling."

He hasn't called me that for a very long time. Apart from being the head of Jansen clan, Master Bowmen was also my uncle. My late mother's older brother. After the death of my parents, he cared for me and took me under his wing. Never married and with his head constantly in books to come up with new spells or magical gadgets, he wasn't exactly the epitome of a parental figure, but he was there to pat me awkwardly on the head when I did something passable. At the same time, he was also there to give me a scowl every time I messed up.

At times I thought he resented me because he'd been kind of forced into looking after a child that wasn't his own, but I'd been happy not to be alone so I ignored it. When I was old enough to demand he buy me things, he came up with that nickname for me: nibbling. Apparently, I was nibbling at his cash. The old man was not happy with me dipping into his bank account.

My anxiety tripled, burning a hole in my gut.

"Who is the client? Do we know?" The minute the questions passed my lips I had a feeling I shouldn't have asked, but it was too late. I bit my lip while I waited for his reply.

"The Magician," he murmured the words way too low and fast.

The tip of my sneaker wedged into a nonexistent crack on the pristine floors. Pitching forward, I almost whacked Master Bowmen across his face with my windmilling arms. Numbness spread through me for that one split second when I pitched forward, my heart stopping and the breath freezing in my lungs, but a strong grip on the back of my shirt saved me with my nose an inch from the parqueted ground. The scent of pine and citrus polish assaulted my nostrils right before I was yanked up, Master Bowmen depositing me on my shaky legs with a glower I'd seen more times than I could count.

Manic laughter burst out of me.

It sounded unhinged and too shrill to my own ears, which made Master Bowmen flinch, his arms shooting to the side and knees slightly bending as if he was about to tackle a crazy person. It made me laugh harder, guffawing in his face with tears prickling the corners of my eyes.

"The Magician." Me gasping the name swiveled his head, his eyes bulging while he made sure no one heard me.

"Stop this instant!" Hissing at me, the old man snatched my arm and manhandled me inside the first door to our right.

It was a linen closet, but whatever.

"Okay, the joke is on me." Swiping the tips of my fingers under my eyes, my mouth opened as wide as my eyelids as I shook my head. "I almost believed you there for a second."

"Listen to me, girl." His fingernails were biting into my skin where he grabbed my upper arms, shaking me until I almost poked my eye out. "We don't have the luxury to wait. This is the time to think of a way to get out of the agreement." My teeth rattled from him jolting me with each word that passed his lips, and my giggles died down in the process.

"You can't be serious." Tugging my arms out of his grabby, knob-knuckled hands, I glared at him. "And what do you mean by *we* need to think of a way out of the agreement? It's you that accepts all the jobs for our clan. Why in all the world did you agree to something so stupid?"

"I wasn't given the option to refuse."

"Do you hear yourself?"

"Charlie—"

"Don't you Charlie me you mother puss bucket!" Stepping into his personal space, I leaned as close to his face as I could get. "What the hell is the matter with you?"

The Magician—the name all of us knew him by—was the leader of the mage faction in our world. The largest in number, and the most powerful thanks to our magic, we were mostly implemented in politics and the government dealings with the human world, which placed the son of a cracknednut above everyone else. Then, there was the shifter faction, which in light of their physical strength and perks they received when they shifted to their secondary forms, monopolized the military and law enforcement. The fae, all types that came from Faerie, with their manipulative prowls and charismatic personas, were the top dogs in any type of media. The demons, who didn't like any of us and didn't want to work with us in any dealings, stayed out of everyone's business, taking it upon themselves to screw with humanity through religion and trade information, but only if you knew where to ask. And of course, the vampires, the cunning bloodsuckers who, because of their longevity, grew roots in finance, instituting the most powerful banks in the world, and by default lording over us all.

Meanwhile, the humans just kept living their ignorant lives, thinking they were safe behind their brick houses and locked wooden doors while everything they considered fiction thrived around them, pulling the strings to control their pathetic lives from behind the scenes. Not that the rest of us were excused from suffering or paying our dues, but we did have more privileges than the mundane. Privileges I was denied at the fragile age of five when the same son of a crackednut that calls himself The Magician killed my parents and justified it by publicly announcing their magic was uncontrollable and unreliable. Since it could out us to the ignorant humans, no one blinked an eye when he killed them in cold blood. I still remembered the look of victory in his eyes as he did it, too.

It was burned into my retinas.

"For the last twenty years, you are the one who has stressed the point that we always have a choice. There are always options if you bother to look for them." With great struggle, I pulled myself from the damning thoughts thrumming through my head and focused on Master Bowmen's face once again.

The smell of laundry detergent and fabric softener drifted around us from the neatly folded linens lining the racks. It was the polar opposite of the murderous thoughts swirling inside me. The floral scent reminded me of open fields and blue cloudless skies, so I sucked in the air, hoping to calm the pulse of magic itching to smite Master Bowmen for daring to tell me this idiocy. The old mage himself had done everything in his power to keep me away from the sights of The Magician.

Yes, he demanded to be called *The* Magician with a capital T.

"You know I have been vouching that your magic is barely there, practically nonexistent." Mesmerized, I watched more lines pop over his wrinkled face, stress pulling the corners of his thin lips down. "Someone has been whispering in his ear, I believe. Maybe this is a test to assure I'm speaking the truth. I might have no choice, but you can refuse to take the mission."

"You'll be okay with me saying no?" I wasn't sure at this point if I wanted to say yes or run for the hills. Nothing good could come from it, that much I knew.

"You can refuse, and I will explain that you are afraid of going after a target as a magicless mage." With a sigh, he searched my face for what seemed like a long time, which left me wondering if he found what he was looking for or not. "Or you can accept and simply try to kill your mark."

My eyebrows crawled all the way to my hairline. "You'd brave a blemish, a black mark on your reputation for me? You want me to fail? On purpose?" I ducked my head to peek at his face since age had brought him a few inches shorter than me. "You said try," I reminded him, that one word more important than any others he'd said. He thought I couldn't do it, so who the hell was the target?

"Of course not." Sounding scandalized, he shoved me a step away from him. "If we don't find a way out of the agreement, you will do the job." With a sharp nod, he tugged his shirt down for no reason.

Color me impressed that I was wrong. He actually looked certain I could do it. And I could. That wasn't the issue. I knew hundreds of different ways to end anyone's life. In theory. But doing it quietly, and with none the wiser was a different matter. For the first time since he found me and told me the grim news that my parents will never open their eyes again, a spark of hope bloomed in the center of my chest, illuminating a dark hole I wasn't aware I had. Maybe I could truly be a productive member of my clan instead of a freak and a screw up. I could prove to all of them that my magic was not a monster to be feared, and that I was good for more than just collecting information to help on their missions.

"You just won't use any magic." And just like that, Master Bowmen killed that tiny light of hope as if he had plucked the wings of a butterfly.

Unwilling to show how much that last comment hurt

me, I squared my shoulders and offered him a stiff nod. Whatever. I was used to being the odd duck. Not like I cared what they thought of me anyway.

It was much harder to swallow the lump in my throat, which was about the size of a fist, the second time.

"Right." Ignoring the pity plastered all over his stupid face, I even smiled. "I can kick a titty chompers butt any day, no magic needed."

"You need to work on your profanities." Grimacing like he smelled something foul, Master Bowmen led us out of the linen closet. I wished everyone would stop saying that. My cursing was perfectly fine.

The fresh, familiar scent of the hallway washed away the last remnants of my pathetic, willowing mood and I decided to actually be excited about the job. Maybe it was exactly what I needed. I'd watched plenty of movies featuring human assassins. If a mundane could become a killing machine without an ounce of magic, so could Charlie Jansen. I just needed to make sure I didn't hesitate like the handful of times I tried to kill before. Easy peasy.

I got this.

"You never told me who the target is," Lost in my own head I didn't see him walking away, so I called after Master Bowmen just as he was limbering to take the corner. "You said I'll find out tomorrow, but I know that you know."

"Always an overachiever." Shaking his head, he couldn't stop himself from chuckling.

He wasn't wrong. I loved being prepared. If I got a head start on this, I might nail it fast enough to make him proud. Now that would be a dream come true. Stick it to all the dimwits that called me a kibitzer.

I yelped when a wedged-up ball of paper plonked me on the forehead, grasping at nothing like a clawing cat scampering not to fall before snatching it midair. With trembling fingers—from excitement not fear—I stretched it open and smoothed the wrinkles out on my thigh.

With a shriek, I jumped back when sparks burst out of my fingertips, the paper burning to ashes. Stumbling back, I bumped a hip and hit my head on the wall, a burst of light blinding my vision. But there was no escaping what I saw. It was permanently tattooed on the back of my eyelids. The blood drained from my face as I slid down the wall, landing hard on my side. The name kept floating in front of my eyes.

Nigel Thatcher

"He wants me to kill the most powerful vampire in existence." Scrambling on my knees, all the air from my lungs tumbled out in a rush as I flung my hair out of my face to see Master Bowmen pinching the bridge of his nose like it pained him to watch me. "Mother trucker!"

Chapter Three

I clutched my beer like it had become my lifeline while lights pulsed and music boomed over the speakers, the bass hitting me like a sledgehammer to the back of the head. Humans were clustered in groups, their sweaty bodies writhing together. Their eyes were glazed over from overindulgence in alcohol, but also from their hormones, which were going into overdrive courtesy of the fae sprinkled among them.

The Cauldron—the last place on earth I wanted to be in—was packed to the brim. One of the very few clubs open to humans and supernaturals alike, it was the hottest place in town. Not that Norfolk, West Virginia was well known for exclusive VIP night clubs. With the Navy docking their boats in the tiny harbor and popping in constantly, it was more of a pub-type city crawling with shifters. Unless you knew where to go, that was. Modern buildings were strategically placed between Victorian style homes, which gave the whole place an artistic feel. What the city lacked from its youth, it made up for with its diversity. If only humans knew the statues of mermaids that were placed at every corner were actually invitations for the siren fae to come and hunt here, and they were way more trouble than they were worth.

With a snort, I leaned on the smooth, polished wood of the bar, swiping my gaze over the bobbing heads on the dance floor, my right leg jiggling up and down in sync with the rhythm. It was some stupid song, one that repeated the same sentence for about four minutes straight. A grin lifted the corners of my mouth when my eyes landed on a petite blonde, who was wiggling her hips my way, both arms in the air as she clutched two beers and fought the crowd to get to me.

"I can't believe you actually came," Tia shouted, probably so she could be heard over the loud music, then she plonked a beer in front of me as she jumped on the barstool at my side. "I was sure you'd pull a Houdini and leave with the excuse that you couldn't find me in the crowd." I totally deserved the stink eye she flung my way. I did lie a few times before, telling her I had come but couldn't find her.

I hated crowds.

"This will shut you up for like what? An hour?" Tilting my head left and right while squinting at her, I pretended to give that serious thought. "Two max."

"You are suck a girl jerk." She huffed as if offended, kicking my shin with her pointy stilettos. Both of us laughed at that.

With her silver wrap dress and her long hair pulled into a tight ponytail that lifted the skin of her cheekbones painfully high, Tia looked ready to be green-eyed arm candy to a number of creatures skulking in the shadowed corners of the VIP section. Too bad for them she was my best friend and off limits. I'd agreed to a crapload of restrictions from Master Bowmen to make sure no one would dare touch her. Even though Tia was human, my uncle was all too happy to oblige as long as he had his hooks deeper into my life. After all, he did tell me not to get close to anyone. "They could be used against you, Charlie. Never offer a weakness when you don't have to." Maybe he kept me at arm's length so I could never become his weakness. Not that I cared.

On this, it was me who took advantage of his overbearing, meddling tendencies.

You could tell we were family.

"What's up?" The smile slipped from Tia's face, and I blinked fast to bring my focus back to her. "I've seen that face twice before and neither time was good."

"I came here to have fun, not talk about my problems." Which was a big fat lie, and I was very good at those. "Plus we are shouting. You really want to talk now?"

Tia eyed me, then the two beers sitting in front of me. With a shake of her head, her ponytail lashed the air at her back and she relaxed her stiff shoulders. Clinking the neck of her bottle off mine, she took a swig and swiveled on the chair to face the dance floor.

"First, I'll get you drunk." Giving me a Cheshire smile, she pointed at the beer in my hand. "Then I'll find out all your secrets, Charlie. I have it all planned out." Her silver-painted nail tapped her temple, and I chortled at the serious look on her face.

"Bring it." Lifting the bottle to my lips, I followed suit, much easier for me turning on the chair in my skinny jeans.

Unlike the rest of the women in the place, I did my best to cover as much skin as possible. For those in the know, finding exposed skin would be a red flag and would make them pay closer attention to find out if I was one of the clans. We hid our markings and tattoos that covered our bodies better than a nun would hide a vibrator she bought from eBay. It showed anyone our level of magic and the strength of our powers, but only if they knew how to read them. Given to us at birth, the marking grew with us, thickening and multiplying as our magic reached its peak.

Hence my long-sleeved, closed-to-my-neck shirt and makeup-free face. The less attention anyone paid me the better. That was one of the reasons I befriended Tia, so she could take the spotlight and I could blend in with the walls. I didn't expect to actually like her. Humans were pawns to be used when needed. That thought made me want to smack myself. I sounded way too much like Master Bowmen.

"Nope, this won't do." Tia jumped off the stool, grabbing my hand and tugging me along with her.

Stumbling after her, I looked like an elephant stomping around compared to her graceful sway, all hips and shoulders. If we were not friends, I would've thought she was one of the fae. But no, she was as human as could be, ignorant of the killer she was dragging to dance with her. *Well technically you are not a killer, yet,* a snide voice inside reminded me that I'm a noob. *Not for the lack of trying,* I shot back, shutting that other voice right up.

Since things were progressing as planned and I hadn't spotted the person I was looking for, I shuffled my feet while Tia danced as if she was in a *Dancing With the Stars* contest. Every eye was on my friend, including the women, although theirs were wary and narrowed, some even spitting venom. Her bubbly personality practically radiated from her skin, pulling everyone to her like planets orbiting around the sun. I slid further back and scanned the club, leaving more space for her to twirl. Being in the middle of the dance floor put me in the perfect position to see everything, including the glass enclosed VIP space on the first floor.

Awareness prickled the back of my neck, but I couldn't spot a single person paying attention to me from above. I felt it though.

Tia shrieked in delight as some new song blared, eliciting responding howls from the frenzied crowd. Ignoring them all, my gaze bounced off the muscly guys in black t-shirts with "Security" written on them in white letters manning the red-carpeted stairs. A couple of the fae gave me curious passing glances, their hungry eyes locking on the grinding bodies. They fed on energy, so this would satisfy their need for a while. I wanted to shout, "You're welcome," but I didn't. I even ignored the shifter with his military buzz cut and muscles over muscles crowding a human chick in the corner, his tongue down her throat while she clawed at his shoulders. None of them were who I was looking for.

I almost throat punched Tia when she snatched my hand and spun under my arm. Waiting until she was stable on her feet, I was about to let go of her when she yanked me around wordlessly demanding I do the same and spin under her arm. My shirt crawled up my torso and I grappled to pull it down, my heart in my throat. Assuring myself that no one was looking at the plain, dark-haired, awkward girl I was, I blew out a sigh while bumping into a few people in my weird twirl. Half a circle under Tia's arm I froze, eyes locked on a face I was hoping to find tonight.

The second he saw me, he bolted.

"Oh, no you don't." Hissing those words I released Tia's fingers.

I left my friend calling my name, tackling people who were in my way as I made a mad dash for the doors. Cursing and snarling followed in my wake, but I only had eyes for the figure disappearing through the double doors ahead of me. My shoulder slammed into the closing door sending mind-numbing pain all the way to the base of my skull. Unable to stop the momentum, I pirouetted out of the club, my limbs outstretched in hopes to regain my balance. My spin ended when I bumped into a woman waiting first in line to enter the club, elbowing her in the boob and going deaf in one ear from her shrill announcement of my embarrassment. I was about to apologize, but I spotted the numbskull I was chasing rounding a corner and disappearing on the side of the club. I left the woman shrieking, words like "bitch" and "what drugs are you on" sprouting from her red-painted lips.

I caught up with the weasel in the barely-lit parking lot, my shoulder still smarting from the kiss it had with the heavy door. Bouncing on the balls of my feet, I pounced on his back and took him down with a very harsh "oomph" from his mouth, which billowed dust right into my face. He sprawled on the grime-covered ground, his arms and legs outstretched like a starfish. Since I was now on his back, I sat on my haunches, grinding my knees into his spine. Coughing, I waved a hand to dispel the cloud of germs floating around my face when he jerked his hips to buck me off him.

"Yew haw, dumbnut." Smacking the back of his head, pressing my knees into his back harder, I grabbed a fistful of hair. "You didn't think you'd actually get away, did you?"

"Let me go, clipper." The demon under me growled, using the street name they called all members of the assassin clans. Since he knew what I was, this one wasn't dumb. It was just my luck to find the one smart demon in town.

Fresh air filled my lungs, the musty, earthy tang of Elisabeth River lapping at the docks across the street unmistakable in each breath I took, clearing the dust clinging to my nostrils. With a large building on one side and the club on the other, we were protected from prying eyes. The demon bucking like a wild bull under me gave me time to catch my breath, and to rub my stiff shoulder to get some of the feeling back. A quick look around confirmed no one followed us here.

"I need information." It actually felt nice sitting on him while he frantically tried to get me off his back, like sitting in a boat as waves slapped the sides of it. It was lulling. *And you are a weirdo.*

"I know nothing." The grinding of his teeth made me cringe.

"You'll break a tooth if you keep doing that, dumbass." I slapped the back of his head again like a mother chastising her toddler. "You will tell me what I need to know or they'll find your carcass sprinkled around here come morning."

"I don't help clippers." But he stopped fighting, his face mushed in the dirt on the ground.

"Good thing I'm not a clipper." *'Yet'* was silent there, but he didn't need to hear that part.

"Lies!" He almost pushed me off him when he surged up in anger. Demons pick up lies like frogs snatching flies. Hardly any are missed.

"I am from a clan, but I'm not a clipper." Pressing his face firmer to the pavement, I leaned closer to whisper in his ear, pitching my voice very low. "Unless you keep talking horseshite and change my status. Tell me demon, do you want to be my first?"

He shuddered despite himself, his skin popping goosebumps everywhere my breath puffed over it. "What do you want?" he finally asked through clenched teeth, and I patted him on the face with a couple of harsh slaps. I followed Jonas one night and saw him getting information from this demon. How he guessed what I was the second his eyes landed on me was something I'd think about later. Now I needed details that hopefully he could provide.

"Where do I find Nigel Thatcher?" The demon stilled under me as if he wished to disappear. "Not the bank, I know I'll never get within a foot of him there."

The problem I faced before actually receiving the file tomorrow was the fact that no one knew what Nigel Thatcher looked like. Oh, people had seen him, but none lived to describe him or even gloat that they met the elusive vampire.

He was a ghost.

None knew his face except The Magician. Coincidence? Me thinks not. Of course the one target they'd give me would be someone no one could find. Maybe that was the main reason Master Bowmen agreed to the mission, because he'd hoped if I couldn't find the target he would say no foul no play. Too bad that in all these years he never spent energy to get to know me better. I was more stubborn than a mule. I'd find Nigel Thatcher if it was the last thing I did.

I might not live after it, but I'd find him.

"Good luck with that." The dumbnut actually chortled, even as he wheezed beneath me.

Magic burst out of my hand, spiraling forward until it formed a single-handed cruciform short sword, ice blue magic mixed with fire red tendrils pulsing over it. The moment I pressed it against the demon's face, my ears felt like they might bleed from his screams. The stench of charred skin drifted up and I scrunched up my nose.

"Nigel Thatcher," I repeated slowly. "Where do I find

him?" The second time I brought the glowing blade to his face, tears streamed from his eyes as he jerked away from it while mumbling incoherent words. "I can't hear you."

"It's rumored that he visits the Black Cat often when he is in town." If I kept frowning, my face would freeze like that. "That's all I know."

"The metaphysical store?" What in the world would a vampire need from a nick-knack store?

"The word is that he's been spending a lot of money on charms and spells. Not just in the store they have here, but in the main one in Vegas." The demon trembled, a weird tone of resignation in his voice.

Jumping off the demon, I stepped back to give him room to escape. My mind was spinning from the unexpected twist. Was it a coincidence that the vampire received his first bullseye painted on his back as soon as he started buying magical items? It was drilled into me from the moment I could understand what words meant that there was no such thing as a coincidence. There were probable and improbable factors, and if they were mutually considered using logic and objectivity they would give us the answer we needed. I was still lost in thought when the demon lifted off the ground and dragged his feet away from me, his head hanging low on his shoulders in defeat.

"I won't tell a soul you said a word," I called after him despite myself.

"You won't have to, clipper. The wind has ears." I held my breath when he looked over his shoulder, his eyes dull. "I'll see you in hell soon enough."

So petulant, this one.

Chapter Four

Keeping to the shadows, I walked at a clipped pace through downtown Norfolk. Pubs and restaurants had their front doors open, making it difficult to blend in. Still, I darted through the bright streaming light hitting the sidewalk keeping my head down and holding my breath. I didn't feel very comfortable being so exposed, and nothing pointed an arrow at your head better than a bright light beaming the side of your face like a spotlight.

Leaving Tia behind at the club meant I'd be getting a thorough tongue lashing the next time she saw me, especially since that wasn't the first time I'd done it to her. A smile tugged at my lips when the image of her glowering with her hands planted on her hips as she told me off comes to my mind. Since she was five foot two to my almost six foot, those arguments were always a lot of fun. In truth, it was like watching a chihuahua bark at a Great Dean.

Veering right on East Plume street, I passed a Starbucks and was instantly reminded of the insatiable need Tia had for caramel macchiatos. I'm definitely bringing her one when I go to see her. That would soften her temper when I apologized.

I trotted down to City Hall Avenue, taking another right on Granby Street. A few people moved around, their attention on their phones and away from me. Black Cat metaphysical store appeared in front of my eyes, taking up more space than needed with its black walls and dark purple door, the tall windows showing all sorts of gimmicky paraphernalia to fool humans. Grace O'Malley's pub next door was a stark contrast with beige and dark green walls, the inviting glow from the yellow light coming through the windows and the cheery Irish tune wafting through the open door softening the menacing vibe from the monstrosity next to it. Finding a good size tree across from the pub at the IRS building, I leaned on it and settled into the darkness. The abandoned parking lot stretched at my back until it was swallowed by impenetrable shadows.

Not that the vampire would show up tonight. No way would I get that lucky. No, I just wanted to get a feel of the place.

A couple exited O'Malley's with their arms linked, both laughing at some inside joke no one was privy to. The man's arm had become a support to the woman, who looked as if all her body weight was inclined on it, and his eyes sparkled in the light of the pub with happiness that he didn't seem to mind her tugging on him as they walked.

Happy.

They were both happy, which had been an unfamiliar feeling to me since twenty years ago when my parents were murdered. With effort, I pulled my eyes away from them, shoving the sadness down before it sunk its claws in me again.

"It's pointless to dwell on things you can't change."

Murmuring under my breath, I kept taking deep breaths. "Keep looking forward, never look back." Repeating my mantra a few times helped.

The street was deserted. After the couple disappeared around the corner nothing but the music, chatter, and shouts from the pub disturbed the night. A cool breeze drifted down and I tugged on my sleeves to pull them over my knuckles, a bad habit I developed at an early age. Focusing on what was important, my mind kept going over the information the demon gave me. What could a vampire with immeasurable power and influence need from magical items? I stared at the black building hard, like it might tell me what I wanted to know. It didn't.

I didn't know much about Nigel Thatcher for one. None of us did. The only information anyone had, came from the vampire himself, and he only gave us what he wanted us to know. A dimwit would figure that out. He was the most powerful supernatural alive, that much I knew. I could see why The Magician would want him gone. The old mage fancied himself at the top, and anyone threatening that spot was an enemy. He was the Pharaoh to rule over us, and since the bloodsucker was pooping on his parade, he finally decided to off him. So how did Black Cat come into the mix?

My feet shuffled and I shifted because my back had gone numb where I'd been pressing it against the tree. Changing positions altered my train of thought. No, the obvious was not the answer, even though it might be part of the reason. I'd bet my life that The Magician was arrogant enough to believe I'd see this as a power play between two major players in our world and stop with that. Just like Master Bowmen, he didn't know me at all, either. I would overthink until I get bored thinking about it. "Leave no stone unturned, Charlie." My uncle's words floated through my mind, making me remember the time I was small enough to sit on his desk while he tinkered with spells.

Harsh lights flashed across my face, and I darted behind the tree, keeping my body in line with the trunk as a car raced down the street. My heartbeat thundered in my ears until the vehicle disappeared down the road, the sound of the engine the last to go. Just as I was about to emerge and take my spot, the door to Black Cat opened, the jingle of the doorbell pulling my attention like it was a siren's song from across the street. This late in the night the store should've been closed, yet a form walked out shrouded in the darkness, closing the door as he or she did. Could I be that lucky that the vampire had been there this whole time?

The person fiddled with the door before lumbering down the set of stone stairs. When both their feet touched the sidewalk, the light from the pub partially uncovered their face from the shadows. A woman in her late sixties with gray hair coiled neatly into a severe bun looked both up and down the road before hiking her purse higher on her shoulder. She was a tiny little thing with a good size bust, which was accentuated by the long, flowing dress she wore that fell to her ankles. From what I was able to see, the harsh lines of her features spoke of a no-nonsense personality I instantly liked. Her face told me "don't waste my time or you'll regret it." While I was studying her, she spun on the heel of her flats and walked away with a determined stride. Without thinking too much about it, I bolted after her.

My feet were silent as a whisper on the pavement, but I noticed the second she knew someone was following her. Her shoulders stiffened and the small steps she was taking lengthened, the hand resting on the strap of her purse tightening into a white-knuckled grip. My heart jumped to the roof of my mouth and I opened my mouth to alert her of my presence before she started running. The last thing I needed was to give some poor old woman a heart attack in the middle of the street.

"What do you want?" She spun around to face me with a scowl.

The tip of my boot hit the uneven pavement and my body lurched forward. Spreading my arms wide to stop the fall didn't help at all, it only made the old woman gasp and take a step back with wide eyes. My own were about to pop out of their sockets as I watched myself fall in slow motion as if I was having an out of body experience. The palms of my hands scraped over the pebbles and my skin shredded when I hit the ground. An embarrassing whimper came out of my chest, all my bones rattling from the impact a second before the air exited my lungs with a whoosh.

"Oh, dear," the old woman whispered above me. "Are you … are you alright child?"

Lifting my head to look at her, her worried face was barely visible through the curtain of my hair. I tried to smile to put her at ease, but it must've looked like a grimace judging by the line forming between her neatly trimmed eyebrows.

"Hi." Groaning the word, I pushed off the dirty pavement, the sting in my palms forcing me to wince. "I didn't mean to scare you, sorry."

"Nevermind you that." Her hand raised as if she was about to reach for me before she let it drop to her side. "That was a nasty fall. Are you sure you are alright?" Indecision flickered over her face for several seconds, but finally she glanced at the black building behind me. "We can go inside the store to get you some water."

The words "I'm fine" died on my tongue, my body stiffening at her offer. I'd only been inside the store twice and it was a long time ago at that. Knowing I wouldn't get an opportunity to check it out without having at least one person following my every step while it was open for business, I swayed on my feet, my hand touching the side of my head.

"I do feel a little dizzy." Her sharp, intelligent gaze searched my face, so I played it smart. "I should be okay in a minute. I don't want to put you out of your way." Then I stumbled a step for good measure.

"Nonsense." Pressing her mouth in a firm line, she took me by the elbow and turned me around. "I can't leave a girl alone at night on the street while she can barely stand on her feet. Let's go."

Oh lady, you have no idea what this girl can do alone at night, I thought, but I didn't say it. Instead, I allowed her to guide me up the stairs and through the door of the store. The copper bell above the door jingled when she opened it, and when she flicked a switch on the side, soft white light cascaded over rows and rows of shelves that covered every available space in the vast room. Bottles of every size and shape glittered around us, statues of gods and goddesses following our progress to the long glass counter at the other end. A register was perched on one corner and tons of crystals sparkled behind the glass of the counter. She pushed me on a tall chair in front of the register.

"Stay here. I'll be right back."

I watched her fling the curtain to the side and listened to her footsteps until they disappeared in the back of the store. When I was sure she'd gone, I jumped off the chair to explore. At first glance everything displayed was made for humans. There wasn't a trace of magic on a single statue, not even in the liquid filling up the fancy bottles. Disappointment hit me like a hammer to the chest. The demon lied. I couldn't see myself coming to this store to look for anything, let alone a vampire who owned the world. Well, their bank accounts at least. A tall wooden cabinet with intricate carvings on the frame and glass protecting the doors caught my attention. The closer I got to it, the more I felt the magic pulsing from whatever was inside. Everything around me faded into nothing and my feet moved on their own.

"Did you find what you were looking for?" I jumped out of my skin when the old woman spoke from behind me.

I twisted around and my eyebrows shot to my hairline. The woman was a few feet away, her eyes narrowed to slits as she clutched an elder wood wand in her hand. The elder was the rarest wood used in wands because of its temperament. It contained very powerful magic and it took remarkable wizardry to keep it for a long time. The old woman was not a mage, though. I would've sensed it when I was close enough on the street.

A witch then. Neither fully human, nor fully magical.

The witches threaded both worlds but fit in none. They were seen as outcasts, exactly like I was from the mage community. I wish I could say it was because I was a witch. And out of all of them, I stumbled on one that could hold an elder wand like a pro.

Mother fudge!

"I can explain." With careful movements, I lifted both hands to my sides in surrender. Also so she could see I hadn't taken anything. "I only wanted to see the store without too many people inside it. I swear it."

"Your words don't mean anything to me clipper," she spat the words at me.

"Oh dear fates, what is it with everyone calling me a clipper tonight?" Exasperated, I flung both my hands in the air forgetting what she holds in hers. "And how do you know what I am?"

The wand twitched.

"I'm not a clipper." The words rushed out of my mouth. "I am part of a clan, but I haven't taken a life. Look at me." With desperation in my tone, I begged her to listen. Especially because that wand could kill us both if she started swinging it around. "If you are strong enough to hold that wand, then you can tell if I'm lying." I had to admit I wasn't sure about that. I did hope, though.

The old woman cocked her head like a bird, the movement sending a shiver of trepidation through me. Did I misjudge her? Did mentioning the wand insult her? It couldn't have. I did know for sure that she wasn't a mage now. A witch was the only thing that fit. Her acute gaze swept me from head to toe and a cunning smile quirked the corners of her lips. My heart plummeted to the floor and splattered between my feet. I swallowed thickly.

"No, you have not." With the creepy smile still on her face, she tucked the wand in the fold of her dress. "But I rarely forget a face." Stepping inside my personal bubble, her head barely reached my shoulder as she patted my face none too gently. "And never a cherubic one like yours, dear."

I flinched.

"Master Bowmen is well I take it?" Like she didn't threaten to blow us both to pieces only second ago, the old woman turned her back on me and stepped to the counter.

"Yeah." Stunned, I followed behind her.

"Bah, cheer up, would you?" She shoved a glass of

water in my hands, and I almost dropped it. "Drink. I had to make sure it's you and not someone with a glamour on."

The water went down the wrong pipe and I sputtered, coughing up a lung and spitting all over her in the process. Her mouth twisted in disgust but she didn't say anything else until I was able to take a breath without dying from it.

"You were expecting me?" Rasping, I wiped my mouth with the back of my hand to remove some of the water dribbling down my chin.

"Well no." She propped a hip on the counter and folded her arms across her chest. "I didn't know when you would come, but the moment Nigel Thatcher came sniffing around the place I figured it was time."

My whole body went numb.

The glass fell from my hand, breaking into thousands of pieces on the tiled floor, soaking both of our shoes.

"You work for The Magician?" It was the only explanation I could come up with since she put me and the vampire in the same sentence. How was it possible she knew before I even received the file?

Who was this woman?

"Oh dear gods, no." She even took a step back as if to distance herself from the vile accusation. "What does that atrocious old fool have to do with this?"

"Nothing." The word was out faster than a bullet. "I just wanted to make sure." I had no idea sure of what exactly but that's not important. My mind was spinning from this conversation. It felt like I was in another universe or dimension.

"Smart." With a nod of approval, she straightened. "I think you can start tomorrow. We don't know when he will come here again."

"Start what?" Maybe she had put something in the

water that made me dumber, and I did feel pretty dumb gaping at her like she was an alien.

"Work, of course." Frowning, she watched me like I was an idiot. Join the club lady. "How else would you cross paths with him?"

The lightbulb went on and I almost jumped to give her a hug. "You want me to cross paths with Nigel Thatcher?"

"Yes." Her chin dipped low and she spoke slowly for the dumbnut I was turning out to be.

"Tomorrow is great, thank you." Not giving her time to change her mind or the drugs she took to wear off, I bolted for the door. "I'll see you tomorrow morning."

"Be here at seven sharp," she called after me.

Holding the door open, I waited for the bell to stop jingling. "I didn't get your name." Peering over my shoulder, my arms prickled with goosebumps when a cunning smile bloomed on her face.

"No, you did not."

What on earth had I gotten myself into now? The bell mocked me with its happy chime when I closed the door and disappeared into the night.

Chapter Five

I showed up at seven sharp in front of the door of the Black Cat blurry eyed and grumpy. I couldn't fall asleep at all the night before, so I ended up tossing and turning in the bed, and when the sheets kept tangling around my legs, frustration hit me hard leaving my eyes wide open. Master Bowmen was not any happier when I woke him up at five demanding the file. Whatever he saw on my face convinced him to spare me the lecture, and he jabbed the folder at my chest, then shoved me away with his knob-knuckled fist before slamming the door of his room in my face. Looking through the file just added to my surly mood. The date on it was for tomorrow, and come morning I had twenty-four hours to kill my target. Apart from that?

Nothing.

It consisted of two pages with general information I could've found anywhere. There wasn't even an eye color, or the shade of his hair on it. I swore I could hear The Magician laughing in my face the longer I stared at the stupid pages. In a fit of anger, I burned the file to dust, almost taking my bed and covers with it. I left the window in my room cracked open in hopes that the stench would be gone by the time I got back.

Twisting the doorknob proved to be yet another obstacle and a clear indicator that this day would not get better. It was locked. Cupping my hand, I mushed my face to the glass to see if there was any movement inside, but nothing stirred in the still dark store. Cars zoomed behind me on the street, and the chatter from the humans rushing about made enough noise to worsen the pounding headache punching my temples. With a defeated sigh, I turned away from the door and plopped down on the top step. Luckily, I was wearing jeans and not the only dress I owned, which I had stupidly considered wearing. It was the nicest thing I owned, though, so I was thankful I didn't have to soil it on the dirty ground.

Fifteen minutes later a woman in her mid-thirties appeared, her face flushed from her mad dash across the street. She waved me in as she was passing and I jogged behind her to keep pace. Dragging me along with her, she moved around the space until she was satisfied before flipping a sign to 'Open'. She didn't even ask me who gave me the job, too happy to send me in the storage room to organize the mess of boxes that almost touched the ceiling. Apparently, they received their new shipment overnight. What a coincidence.

From wooden crates to Amazon boxes, the towers leaned awkwardly like the leaning tower of Pisa, making me edgy every time I reached for the top one. I lined them all up with a clenched jaw and minimal muttering under my breath. The old woman said I'd cross paths with my target, but that surely wouldn't happen if I was stuck in the storage room. By the time I was done, the same woman who opened the store—Mary Alice was her name—came to tell me my shift was over and I could go home. I guessed I didn't get to have a break. Modern day slavery it seemed.

Blowing out a breath, I wiped the sweat off my forehead with the sleeve of my shirt while looking at the smooth lines I created by stacking the boxes. I made the storage room as organized as a whistle while my life was flipped on its head and thrown into chaos. Being here helped with nothing apart from calming my nerves and apprehension. I didn't learn anything new about the bloodsucker, nor did he mysteriously appear out of thin air. I wasted half a day where I could've found someone to point me in the right direction.

"Keep looking forward, never look back." The mantra sounded sour on my tongue.

"That's a nice way of looking at things." The old woman was resting against the doorframe, and who knew how long she'd been standing there. I was letting this mission get to me, and in return I'd get killed for not paying attention.

"If you say so." If I sounded upset, that was because I was. Not with her. With myself. Mostly.

"You don't like the job?" There was a mocking tone in her voice that rubbed me the wrong way, so I whirled on her.

"What's your game lady?" My magic surged, the two blades glinting from the swinging lightbulb in the windowless room. I brought the sharp edge with ice blue magic and fire red tendrils close to her face, but she didn't even blink. "I need to find the vampire before dawn tomorrow, and here I am organizing your boxes. Want to share who put you up to stopping me from getting my mark?"

She smiled.

Not a cunning one like the night before, or even a crazed one since she was a second away from giving Death a hug. It was a proud smile, as if I'd proven myself worthy in her eyes by threatening her life. That was when I noticed that the end of the long hallway had turned deathly silent. Mary Alice had left for the day.

My eyes narrowed on the old woman.

"So you want to see Nigel Thatcher by dawn tomorrow?" Her face tilted to the side, which put her too close to my blade. My hand flinched and her gaze sharpened at the barely perceptible movement.

That was why I made a terrible assassin. I couldn't bring myself to kill anyone without good reason.

With a groan, I made the short swords disappear, my shoulders slumping. "Yes, I do." Scrubbing a hand over my face, I pushed past her while waving an arm behind me. "Your storage is immaculate. You're welcome."

"He will be at the Glass Light Hotel and Gallery tonight." The old woman spoke from behind me as I reached the black curtain separating the back offices from the store. I didn't hear her move and I'd been listening for it. "The one next door."

Turning to face her, I didn't let myself hope that she was telling the truth. "You never told me why you are helping me." The night before, I refused to look a gift horse in the mouth, but things had changed since then.

"I have my reasons." Shrugging a shoulder, she watched me with her face tilted up, completely at ease facing off a mage like myself.

Not many can say the same.

"And you know Mater Bowmen how exactly?" It served me right for not mentioning her when I went looking for the file.

"We are old acquaintances, your uncle and I." The familiar shiver of dread crawled up my spine and clawed at the back of my skull.

"Don't play games with me, old woman. I can kill you right here, right now, and no one will know what happened to you." Taking a step close enough to loom over her small frame, I let my magic come forward and I knew the moment she saw it streaking through my irises. For all her bravado, the skin on her face paled slightly, her breath hitching in her lungs. "Who would miss an old woman, huh? I can stop your heart with a touch. No evidence of foul play as far as the humans are concerned."

She shook the fear off like a cloak, her shoulders snapping back enough to widen my eyes. "You don't scare me, Charlie Jansen. Keep your tricks for those stupid enough to not understand what a valuable creature you are." One trembling finger poked me in the breastbone. " If you want to find Nigel, I suggest you go and change. You don't want to be thrown out of the hotel for looking haggard, do you?"

The old woman shouldered her way past me and I was too stunned to stop her. I watched her disappear behind the curtain with my mouth parted.

"And if I were you, I wouldn't go looking for him in penthouses or fancy rooms." Her voice floated to my ears through the fabric separating us. "He didn't stay hidden this long by flashing his wealth in everyone's face." I snapped out of my stupor just as I thought I heard her murmur, "Unlike some idiots we both know."

I dashed into the store almost ripping the curtain in the process, but there was no sign of her anywhere. Darting between the shelves and looking behind things yielded no answer to where she was hiding from me. The copper bell on the door stayed silent, which was the only proof she didn't leave through the front entrance. After a good tenminute search, I gave up, standing in the middle of the store with my hands propped on my hips.

"Fudge brownies!" I was glad no one could see me stomping my foot as I hissed at the empty store.

The air conditioning turned on, blasting me with cold air and rustling my hair around my face. The sweat soaking up my shirt and skin made me shiver involuntarily, and I hugged myself while rubbing my arms. I could've sworn the old witch was doing it on purpose to get me moving out the door. Who in their right mind would leave a person they'd only met once alone in their store? I could be a thief for all she knew. Or an assassin.

Oh, wait. I am.

Snorting at that, I let myself out, closing the door behind me to the happy tune of the bell. It took me no time at all on my poor, abused scooter to reach the house. The closer I was, more anxious I became. There are always around thirty people at one time in the large mansion. Each one of them a silent killer, lurking around and waiting for someone to step out of the line, especially me. They'll want nothing more than to remove me from their way. Avoiding everyone was hard, but I rushed up the stairs to my room like my butt was on fire. Tugging off my jeans, which were sticking to my legs from sweat, I jumped on one leg to the bathroom. Trail of clothing was left in my wake to the shower but I didn't care. My skin was stinging from the harsh rubbing I gave it, and in no time at all, I was in my black pants and shirt with a hood, the trademark uniform all of us wear when on a job. Shrugging a jacket on to make myself look less like an assassin and more like a goth the humans would give a wide berth to, I slid out of the front door before they noticed I'd come back. Long years of skulking around my home came in handy at times like this. The eerie silence in the house left me unnerved and the sigh was too heavy when it whooshed out of me.

My arms were trembling from excitement as I gripped the handles of the sputtering scooter down the streets of Norfolk, and when I reached the parking lot of the IRS building, I killed the engine maneuvering the bike around by pushing with my feet Flintstone style. The hotel from across the street looked inconspicuous. The Black Cat on the other end of the street looked menacing as usual, with the pub between them merrily chiming its tunes. Combing my fingers through my long black hair, I hoped my attempt actually made it look somewhat presentable and not like a rat's nest from the wind whipping it around my face. Zipping my jacket to cover my hood and face covering, I strode across the street, barely missing a car that almost clipped me.

"Don't get yourself killed before you complete this mission, Charlie." Crazed laughter bubbled out of me as I reached the front of the hotel.

A man dressed in a nicely pressed suit walked out, giving me an uninterested passing glance. I filled my lungs with air to bursting before releasing it slowly through pursed lips. Not wanting to linger on the street for too long, I entered the hotel with an even stride, avoiding eye contact with those lingering in the lobby. My focus was on the bold guy manning the long polished desk, rubbing at his beer belly while staring at the screen of the computer in front of him. A golden badge was sitting on the left side of his crème colored shirt, a name scribbled on it in black letters.

I had to bite on my tongue when I passed a pink statue of spun glass in the form of a rabbit. What in the world kind of joke was this? The most elusive bloodsucker in the world hung out in hotels clustered with rabbits made of glass? How deep does the hole go? It was almost as if the fates were plainly laughing in my face. "Run little rabbit, run.' I could just hear their mocking laughter in my head.

"I need a room." I barely reached the front desk before getting the guy's attention.

"We are booked out." He didn't even grace me with a glance, his eyes glued to the screen.

"I'll pay double." How, I had no idea, but he didn't need to know that either.

"We are booked out." Still not even a flick of his eyes my way.

I leaned to the side to see his solitaire game pulled up. I guess I was doing something right in my attempt to not be noticeable if he didn't pay me any attention. Knowing I'd have to find a different way in instead of knocking him out which would've been bad business that night, I swiveled my head to search for another way to the rooms. The bar to the side was calling as if it had a neon sign pointing at it, the dim lighting and twinkling lights around the long slab on the bar pulling me in. Pushing off the front desk, I walked across the lobby, my feet sinking in the thick oriental rug stretched in the middle of the gleaming floor, straight in through an open arched way, passing another glass rabbit inside it, though this one was blue. Modern paintings were placed on the walls, a nice contrast to the dark wood and brown tones of the upholstery on the sectioned booths lining the walls. There were two exits, one on each side of the indoor café and a door marked "employees only" just to the right of the bar.

Filing everything in my head for later in case I need it, I found myself a secluded barstool at the far left corner that offered a clear view of the whole place. The bartender, much better mannered than the desk clerk, reached me just as I jumped on my seat. Dressed in a white shirt and black vest, he looked presentable, if not a little stiff. It could've been his glower that made me think that, too.

"What can I get for you this evening, Miss?" I gave him what I hoped was a shy smile, trying not to wrinkle my nose at his nasally tone.

"I'll have a glass of chardonnay, please."

"We have a few options for the white wines—"

"Surprise me." The glare I got for having the audacity to cut him off disappeared. He perked up at that, no doubt seeing dollar signs from the ignorant woman as he rushed to get my drink.

Seductive tune was chiming through the speakers, the sultry voice of the singer caressing my senses just right to drop my stiff shoulders down. It'd serve me right if he brought a hundred dollar wine glass, but I needed to find a target who would be the ticket I needed to enter the belly of this hotel without looking suspicious. The last thing I needed was for the vampire to bolt.

Three men and two women were occupying a booth across from the bar, all of them looking like they'd rather be anywhere else but sitting in the company they held this evening. An older couple dressed to the nines were having a dinner on one of the tables, and two other men, on a business meeting judging by the lively conversation and papers scattered between them, took up the third table. That was all I had to work with, so when the bartender brought the wine, I chugged half of it down without tasting it. A headache was starting behind my eyes, the low beat of it thrumming at my temples.

My hand lowered the glass slowly when a guy in his thirties b-lined for the bar like he was on a mission, waving the bartender from the entrance. His button down shirt looked wrinkled and the knees of his dress pants were ballooning out like he borrowed a pair from a larger man. A smile stretched my lips as I twirled the stem of the wine flute between my fingers. Luck might've just turned her blessings on me tonight.

I found my ticket in.

Chapter Six

"He doesn't look like your type." The smooth baritone coming from right behind me raised goosebumps over my arms.

Unlike with the old woman, I knew he was there. For some ridiculous reason, I had a feeling he wanted me to hear him approach me. I knew it was silly because whoever he might be, he was human. It could've simply been the loud, clumsy way humans like to stomp around as if announcing their presence to the earth and not an intentional thing on his part. There wasn't even a trace of supernatural in the guy if you managed to ignore the tone of his voice. Now that was magic all on its own, and it brought everything female in me to the forefront. It took great effort not the show how he affected me when I glanced over my shoulder.

Let's just say I was very grateful I was sitting down.

He had a stupidly handsome face. I thought "stupidly" because I hadn't seen a fae or any of my kind with a chiseled jaw like his, high cheekbones sharp enough to cut glass, a straight nose proportional for his face, and eyebrows arched regally over eyes the color of stormy skies framed in thick, dark lashes the same color as his mussed hair. With shoulders broad enough to give his dark blue t-shirt a run for its money, the sculpted muscles of his pecks and abdomen shamelessly outlined through the thin material, the guy left me speechless for a long moment. Casual jeans that screamed of money hung on his narrow waist, wrapping tightly over powerful thighs. Realizing that I was bluntly checking him out—and he stood there allowing me to take a good look—I snapped my eyes from his loafers back to his face.

He smiled, two dimples popping up on the stubble-covered cheeks.

I barely held back a pained groan, his perfection making me distrust him the same second.

"Neither are you." The smile fell from his face. "Go away."

Turning back to face the bar and the shelves lining the mirrored wall full with all kinds of bottles I'd never be able to pronounce, I cradled the wine between my hands. If I was gripping the flute harder than necessary it wasn't anyone's business. The human unnerved me more than if The Magician was standing in front of me demanding my head on a pike. What the hell was the matter with me the last two days?

"That's not a wine for a woman like you." Ignoring my dismissal, he reached over my shoulder and plucked the glass from my hand.

I turned a frosty glare at him, one that had made many men cower at my feet, until now.

The son of a biscuit eater smirked.

He smirked!

"He will charge you for top quality wine while you drink this piss." Taking the seat next to me—uninvited I might add—he proceeded to ignore my fuming.

I hated everything about him, including the stupid British accent that appeared with the last words that passed his full bow-shaped lips. A shiver made me twitchy on the barstool. I didn't like his accent. Not one bit.

"Fiddle sticks!" I hissed under my breath, turning as far away from him as I could.

"I beg your pardon?" From the corner of my eye, I could see him grinning at me, which only made me grind my teeth.

"Listen, dumbnut." I had to catch myself on the bar when I turned to him sharply, otherwise I would've face-planted in his lap and that was definitely a no go. My face burned from embarrassment, while his smile grew. "I don't know you. I don't want to get to know you." Those lips parted making me lose my train of thought for a second. Thankfully, I recovered in time to stop him from unleashing that deep voice that scrambled my brain. "I'm not looking for company, so go away or I will call security."

There, that should've had him running for the closest exit.

"The name is Blade." The human had the gull to wink at me with those stupid eyes.

"I don't care."

"Should I guess yours?" Cocking his head to the side, he pursed his lips.

"No."

"Anabel."

"Go away."

"No, I suppose it wouldn't be something as ordinary as that."

"You have a serious problem dude."

"Ah!" Excitement made his gray eyes sparkle. "Gertrude."

"What?" He laughed at the horrified look on my face, throwing his head back and closing his eyes. I gaped at him like I was an idiot.

I also wanted to slap him.

"You should've seen your face." Chuckling, he slapped his hand on the bar, which got him a nice glare from the bartender, though he ignored it, of course. The human must be on some drugs or something.

I eyed him suspiciously.

"I assure you I'm not certified." Another wink.

"Yet." I grinned when the smile fell from his lips.

"You should smile more often, darling. It makes your face glow."

It took a moment for what he said to register in my brain. My heart sank to my feet when the guy, who I had pegged as my ticket to enter the rooms of the hotel, swallowed his drink in one gulp and left the bar. No wonder Master Bowmen didn't want to give me targets. I couldn't even get inside a building. I was a horrible assassin and a disgrace to my clan.

"Hey." The knuckle of a crooked finger lifted my chin, my gaze locking on the stormy gray of the human's eyes. "I had no intention of upsetting you, darling. I'll leave you to enjoy your drink." Sliding off the barstool while keeping his gaze on me, I noticed the regretful look in his eyes and for some preposterous reason, tears prickled the corners of my eyes.

"It's fine." Shifting my head to the side, I let the hair fall over my face so he couldn't see the emotion in my eyes.

"Have my drink and anything the lady orders tonight

billed to my room." The human spoke and my head jerked back leaving me staring at his profile while he addressed the bartender. "I apologize again for the intrusion of your privacy." He told me after returning his attention to me.

My heart was trying to punch a hole through my chest. Could I pull it off? Manipulate him to take me inside the hotel and be strong enough to ditch him the first chance I got? My logical brain was desperately screaming "no," but somehow, I convinced myself that I could do it.

I gave him a timid smile.

His eyes narrowed slightly.

"Well, you made sure the one who wasn't my type got away." Why in all the world I sounded breathless was beyond me. "At least stay now so I don't have to drink alone."

"I wouldn't want to bother you more than I already have." The intensity of his gaze prickled my awareness, but I blinked and it was gone.

I searched his face, but he stood there waiting for my decision as if he had all the time in the world. He didn't. If he agreed to take me to his room and resisted me walking away before we reached it, the poor human would be dead before the night was over. He had zero time to play with on his hands. Pretty face or not, tonight was not his night.

I gave him another smile. "I'm sure." The corners of his lips twitched and he settled back next to me. "I'm not giving you my name, though."

"A woman of mystery." Placing an elbow on the bar, he cupped the side of his face and turned his torso to face me. His bicep bulged, drawing my eyes to the smooth skin there. "I rather like mystery, as well as women. The two together is a combination I cannot resist."

Butterflies erupted in my stomach.

"Less talking, more drinking." I waved a hand in his face, which made him laugh good-naturedly. "We are wasting valuable time here."

"What's the rush, darling?" But he flicked his wrist, getting the bartender's attention immediately. Couldn't blame the poor shmuck.

"I turn into a pumpkin at midnight." The human barked out a laugh, making me giggle stupidly.

"Not your carriage then? It is you that turns into a pumpkin? I must see this phenomenon." I watched his profile as he ordered our drinks, a smile plastered on my face.

I might be a dead woman walking come morning, but at least I'd feast my eyes on this perfection of humankind. They should make more of him, I decided. It'd be cruel to women of any kind, human and supernatural alike, to have just one like him. As if reading my mind, his head turned and the hunger in his stormy eyes took my breath away.

"You are British?" Talking about him would stop any questions aimed my way and hopefully give me enough time to stop feeling flustered. Men love talking about themselves from what I know about them. I lived in a house that was mostly full of males after all. Humans can't be that different.

"Among other things," was his elusive reply.

"You don't want to share?" Taking the glass of wine he offered, I startled when his fingers brushed mine. Icy shards stabbed me at the center of my chest and I almost dumped the wine on his jeans.

"Easy there." He steadied my hand, the creeped-out feeling I got a second ago nowhere to be found.

I was losing my mind.

"It's been a long day." Avoiding his gaze, I sipped the

chilled beverage, its floral undertones bursting on my tongue. "Mhm, this is a good wine. Excellent choice, my friend."

"Thank you kindly," Blade answered primly. "But friend is not what I'd like to be."

The back of my throat felt like invisible feathers were tickling it, so I drank some more of the delicious wine to hide my reaction. The damn human would be the death of me. This was what happened when you suffered a dry spell, exposing yourself to a long stretch of self-inflicted celibacy. You saw a hot guy and you turned dumber than a box of rocks. Way to go, Charlie.

Blade was sipping his scotch with deceptive nonchalance. A human wouldn't have noticed the focused intensity he had centered on me, illusively looking around the café while I felt his acute awareness brushing my skin. If he was a supernatural, I would've pegged him for a jaguar shifter by the way his entire body was relaxed while it was coiled to strike the moment you least expected it.

"And what would you rather be?" I asked him when I was sure I wouldn't sound like a girl with a crush.

He leaned closer, invading my personal space and bringing with it the scent of musk and male. My nostrils flared in sync with his, and I wouldn't have been surprised if the rest of the people in the place didn't start sweating from the pheromones drenching the air. Everything about Blade screamed of sex: the way he moved, the way he talked, and the way he held himself. A viral male in his prime. *Down girl.* I reminded my libido to calm down.

"Would you join me in my room?" He held me prisoner with the storm brewing in his irises. "I'd rather show you what I'd like to be than waste breath on useless words."

Oh how I wished that this one time they hadn't given

me a target, that I could just be the usual klutz I was. That I could be the embarrassment of the clan. I would've taken him up on his offer and had him out of the offensive clothing hiding his body from me before he blinked an eye. I could hope he stayed in town longer and I'd be able to find him after dealing with the bloodsucker. And that thought was some major motivation to eliminate my target stat.

I placed the wine on the bar gently, and he followed each move I made like a hawk. "Lead the way, Blade."

Sliding off the barstool, I let my chest brush off his. The deep growl rumbling through him made me want to run so he could chase me. What an absurd thing to think, but he took my hand and tugged me along before I could analyze it too closely. Leaning slightly back, I shamelessly checked out his butt, the firm glutes making me groan with regret. He was a few inches taller than me, which only added to his appeal.

My life was horrible. It was official.

The guy was on a mission, his long strides eating up the space across the lobby. Too happy to oblige, I followed step for step while thinking up ways to shake him off when we reached his hotel room. A couple of women turned as if to follow him as well, their eyes hungrily roaming over him regardless of who was watching. I couldn't blame them, but I didn't understand the need to hiss like a feral cat in their face. This whole night was nuts.

Blade yanked the door to the stairs open, and I didn't think too much about it before rushing in after him. My boot bumped the thin wooden strip raised above the floor and I slammed into his back, which propelled us both into the closed-up space, the door clicking shut behind us.

He twisted around, hitting the opposite wall with his back and curling both his arms around my waist before tugging me to his chest. I had a second to widen my eyes before his mouth slammed against mine.

It was an urgent, hungry kiss that stole the oxygen from my lungs, and I clawed at his shoulders to get him closer. His tongue pushed past my lips to tangle with mine, and I moaned desperately in his mouth spurring him on. His hands were everywhere, running over my back and sides, his strong fingers grabbing my butt and pulling me close enough for his hard erection to poke my belly. Insanity had me in its clutches long enough to know I would never find a man who would make me lose control of my senses like this with just a kiss as long as I lived.

It was enough to bring my brain back to the present.

I slowed down our urgency, pulling back and savoring the taste of him. Blade was everything I didn't know I wanted, and I kept my eyes squeezed tight while the palm of my hand slid from the back of his neck, over his shoulder, and stopped to rest on top of his left pectoral. His hand cupped the side of my face as he followed suit, enjoying me as much as I was enjoying him. My heart shriveled in my chest when I sent the magic zapping through my palm. His body stiffened, a surprised grunt the only sound he made before slumping against me. I prayed to anyone who would listen that I didn't do any permanent damage. When my fingers found his pulse, my knees buckled and I almost dropped him from the relief washing over me.

"Sorry." Mumbling the apology, I turned him around and lowered him to the ground right at the door. Arranging his arms and legs to look like he fell asleep from too much drinking, I flipped the metal lever and locked the door. It'd give me time to search for the vampire, especially if it was up to the clerk at the desk to unlock it. That guy would let the hotel burn before he looked away from that screen. I felt like a creep when I brushed the hair that had fallen over his forehead, but I couldn't help it. "I wish I met you tomorrow Blade, or the day after that." With one last look at his handsome face, I took the stairs two at a time.

I had a bloodsucker to find, and he would pay for my sexual frustration, too.

Chapter Seven

With all my senses on high alert, I searched the floors of the hotel like a bloodhound on a trail. Ducking left and right to avoid people coming out or going in their rooms was not that big of a deal. Not many moved around at this hour. Giddiness gave me a burst of speed as I envisioned Master Bowmen's shocked face when I returned and told him I completed the mission. That will show the old man that theory is as good as practice. I wasn't just a nerd, I was a killer, too.

I felt the first sign of magic on the fourth floor.

Picking up magical items would be Nigel Thatcher's downfall in more ways than one. Vampires could hide their signatures, especially one as old as him, if they chose to do it. Objects on the other hand cannot be hidden from someone like me. My feet slowed as I moved from door to door, looking over my shoulder occasionally to make sure no maid or a late partier saw me lurking in the hall. The carpeted floor added one more assurance to my task, my feet gliding over it like I wasn't even there. I stopped at the door with the number 507 stamped on it, the magic from behind the closed entrance pulsing like a heartbeat, calling my name. Tugging the hood of my shirt from my jacket, I tucked my hair under it, pulling it over my head. The face covering was next, and I attached it to the opposite side to protect my identity from the target. The only thing visible were my eyes after all that. I stiffened my spine and touched the electronic lock frying it's mechanism before pushing the door open on silent hinges and stepping into the dark room.

Being in the room felt like being inside a tomb.

The curtains were pulled tight over the windows, an assurance no light would penetrate inside come morning just how the bloodsuckers like it. I waited at the door until my eyes adjusted to the darkness before moving further inside. An occasional honk came from the outside street, as well as a hushed giggle from the hall before I heard a door shut across from this room. The magic from whatever the vampire had found was luring me like a siren's song. If I had any spare time after I killed him, I'd look for it. Maybe replacing some of the things I destroyed when I burned down the infirmary would get me a bonus point in the clan. Or I could add it to the collection of small things I took from all the dimwits in my clan who thought nobody could get through their doors or wards. Some assassins they were. They might call it stealing. I called it petty revenge for calling me names. And none of them knew who was taking their things.

Feeling confident that it was safe to move, I finally stepped into the simple room, passing the door to the small bathroom on my left. I could see the shadowed form of a flat screen TV hanging on a wall across from a king-sized bed. A bolted desk was pushed to one side with a single armchair next to it. Apart from the two bedside tables one with a large vase stuffed with flowers to bursting on it, there was no other furniture in the room. Thick, heavy scent of roses permitted the air, saturating it.

My gaze focused on the lump on the bed last.

The vampire was dead to the world—pun intended—the covers tucked all the way to the back of his head. Slowing my breathing, which slackened my heartbeat as well, I glided over the soft rug until I stopped at the side of his mattress, my knees barely brushing against it.

The guilt of killing him without him having a chance to fight for his life almost doubled me over, but I kept reminding myself that he was as bad as The Magician. Both of them were manipulative, cold-blooded killers whose deaths would make both worlds—human and supernatural alike—much better. And The Magician, that son of a cracked nut might kill me too if I didn't do what he asked me to do. I had no delusions that I would escape unharmed whatever he had planned by asking this target to be given to me. No, there is an ulterior motive in this train wreck of a situation, I just need to figure it out before he makes his move. With that in mind, I let the short swords slide free, the magic eerily illuminating the dark room in blues and reds.

Silver hair peeked from under the covers, allowing me to see the vampire sleeping with his back to me. Like I needed anything else to make me feel guiltier. I'd be literally stabbing him in the back. It served the bloodsucker right. Knowing I wouldn't do it if I lingered and stayed in my head, I cocked my arm back and slammed it into the part of his back protecting his heart so fast, a muscle overextended on my shoulder sending a sharp pain through my spine and neck. My sword passed through everything like butter, not even the scent of burning flesh floating up to my face.

I blinked.

Yanking the blade out with a flinch, I grabbed a handful of the covers and flipped it off the bed. Lumps of pillows met my glare, one of them with scorched feathers puffing out of it and a silver wig rolled down on the sheets. My whole body stilled and numbness spread like a wave through my limbs.

The vampire knew I was coming.

White noise filled my ears, and I could hear my blood rushing through my veins. Spinning around, I threw the covers I was still clutching to the side. Eyeing the door, I had a feeling if I left right then I'd walk straight into the bloodsucker's hands. He was close, waiting to catch me when I run. That left me one option, and it wasn't one I was too crazy about but baggers can't be choosers.

I wanted to live more.

I rushed to the window and yanked the curtain open.

"I see you found the room."

I stumbled back in shock.

The old woman from the Black Cat was leaning her butt on the windowsill, hidden like some creep behind the curtain, the light from the streetlights and the city casting a weird glow around her like a halo. Her entire body flickered like a picture with bad reception, and she morphed into a young woman around my age with silver hair that was still styled in a no-nonsense bun. The elder wood wand was casually clutched between her fingers.

Panic took over, and it made the next decisions for me.

Spinning around, I took one step for the front door before a switch was flipped and bright light burned my retinas. I blinked fast to force my vision to return to normal, then gasped in terror when I saw Blade walking through the door.

"Get out of here, Blade."

My hand froze midair as I reached for him when his gray eyes locked on my face. A small smile lifted the corners of his full mouth and two sharp fangs peeked from under his upper lip.

"You." The whisper was wrenched out of my chest.

"Hello, Charlie Jansen from the Jansen clan." Nigel freaking Thatcher strode in the room with his hands tucked in the pockets of his jeans and a glint of a dumbnut wafting out of him.

"You ... you ... asphole," I stuttered, wanting to call him every ugly name under the sun but coming up with none of them.

One of his sculpted eyebrows curled like a pointed arrow.

"You see, darling, I think you found yourself in a pickle." I stood still while he circled me like a jungle cat who cornered a mouse.

"Pickle is a sour vegetable." Blurting out the first thing that came to my mind, my fingers were twitching to wrap around his neck and strangle him.

"Is it now?"

"If you aren't sure, then I can't help you there. Intelligence is genetic, something your bloodline obviously lacks." The fact that he outsmarted me and had me trapped was not lost on me. I just chose to ignore it.

His chuckle infuriated me as much as it turned me on. I'd definitely lost my mind on my way here. The old, now young witch, giggled at my back.

"I really like her." The traitor who sent me here gushed at the vampire, making my jaw hurt from grinding my teeth.

"Yes"—He circled back stopping within a foot of my face—"there is something about her, isn't there Selina?"

"Definitely something special." She parroted, still glued to the window. Maybe if I was fast enough I could push her off the fourth floor. We'd see how she liked it when her head cracked like a melon on the street.

"I have a proposition for you, Charlie Jansen." If looks could kill, my glare would've melted the skin off his face when he tugged the hood off my head and speared his fingers through my hair, arranging it around my shoulders. I remained still, not giving him the satisfaction of showing how much his nearness unsettled me.

"Saying my full name doesn't make you sound intimidating. It's kind of lame."

"Is that so?"

"Can you think of a different question because that one is boring."

His grin stretched wider, sending a tendril of fear right through my heart. His fangs were either growing or I was hallucinating, the sharp tips of them peeking from under his upper lip. Now that he wasn't hiding his nature, his power battered my insides like a raging bull. I expected to start bleeding from my ears and mouth at any moment if he kept it up. The only thing stopping me from calling on my swords and plunging them in his chest was the awareness of the elder wood wand at my back. One flick of that wand and they wouldn't be able to collect me with a magnifying glass.

My eyes narrowed on Nigel's face.

"Don't even think about it, Charlie." The up tilt of his lips didn't falter for a second. "I don't want to hurt you."

"Right." The snort that came from me had a line forming between his brows, puckering his forehead. With no way out—still breathing that was—I blew a raspberry in his face. "What do you want, Margie?" When confusion twisted his perfect, stupid face, I laughed humorlessly. "Thatcher, like Margaret Thatcher, the human woman. So Margie it is."

The bloodsucker shook his head like he was dealing with a child. See how much that bothered me. I had lots of fiddle sticks to give, but none would be given to him and his dimwitted butt. Regardless of how firm and tight said butt was. *Stop it Charlie.* I had to physically shake those thoughts out of my dumb brain, which made Nigel peek at me from between his long lashes to check if there is something mentally wrong with me.

"For someone not willing to take a life, you sure are fast to rush into situations like this." The bloodsucker had the grace to mock me.

I really wanted to laugh.

I shook my hands to return some feeling in them instead.

"I have killed before." I had nothing to prove to him, but the words were out before I could stop them. It was too late to backpedal when interest sparkled in his intent gaze.

"You are full of surprises, Ms. Jansen. And who was it that you killed? Do tell." With his upper body leaning forward, Nigel watched me as if he could see all the way to my soul.

My mouth dried up.

The sound of a door slamming in the hallway made me jump a foot off the ground.

The numbnut smirked.

"That's none of your business." Pushing the words through clenched teeth, I glared at him.

"Practice dummies do not count …"

"It was a living being."

"... no matter how much you wish it to be so." The corners of his lips lifted. My stomach somersaulted before it dropped to my feet. "Who, Ms. Jansen. Whose life did you take with that delicate hand of yours?"

"There is nothing delicate about me you son of a biscuit eater." My palms itched to slap the growing smile right off his stupidly handsome face.

"You are ravishing, Ms. Jansen, but we will get to that later." The blood sucker was having way too much fun, while Selina sat at the window as if she was mute, the elder wand twirling in her hand as if she was enjoying the show. "Who did you kill?"

"A squirrel, okay?" If I would've shouted my reply any louder all the humans five stories down would've heard me.

Nigel blinked at me. "A squirrel?"

"It was eating my fruit." I cringed inside at my defensiveness, though I sharpened my glare and dared him with my look to say something.

Throwing his head back, he laughed.

I gaped at his upturned face as Selina's giggles reached my ears as well.

I didn't have time for this type of crazy.

"The proposition?" I hated that my hand was trembling when I whirled it in his face. He didn't even flinch from the movement although if he knew my clan and the magic we possessed he should've had a lot more space between us. "Although you already propositioned me once tonight. We both know how that one ended."

Hunger darkened his gray irises, his pupils spreading to overtake the color. His nostrils flared and his upper body leaned closer, something he didn't do on purpose if I was to take a wild guess. He caught himself and stiffened, those eyes turning into slits as if what he'd been doing was somehow my fault. If he wanted to blame me, he could get in line.

"There are two ways out of this for you." All teasing and humor disappeared from him, sucking up all the oxygen in the room, which made me think I imagined the good natured teasing from earlier. At least he dropped the subject about the poor squirrel, thank the fates. "You die and your clan gets picked off one by one until no one is left and even the memory of clan Jansen is erased from our history for your failed attempt to kill me."

"The night is still young." I muttered under my breath.

That same eyebrow cocked when he paused as if I was dumb enough to repeat what I said twice. Ignoring my outburst, he grinned at me. "Or you can do a small task for me and we can pretend none of this happened. What do you say, darling?"

"I say the next time you call me 'darling' you better be ready to kill me because I'm going to stab you in the eye. The right one." It's the one he'd been winking with all night. I really wanted to cripple him there since it was a weapon he could use to weaken my knees. His knowing smile told me he knew why I picked the right one as well.

"Very well." A regal incline of his head followed, and it was as if he was holding court. "I will refrain from using endearing soliloquy, Charlie. Or do you prefer Ms. Jansen."

"Ms. Jansen will do until further notice, thank you." I shot back at him primly with a sniff. If he wanted to use words that were tongue twisters, I could act posh, too. I lifted my nose up, and if I'd gone any higher it would've hit the tall ceiling. His lips twitched again at my display of arrogance.

"Do you need a moment to make the decision. Ms. Jansen?"

"Are you going to leave the room if I do?"

"No."

"Then I'm fine, thanks."

I really didn't want to agree to anything without knowing what kind of mess he was going to drag me into. Something was fishy here but the adrenalin rushing under my skin was scrambling my brain and I couldn't think. At this very moment, I was up to my eyeballs in trouble. No need to add more carrots to the mishmash. There goes my brain following the train of thought after seeing the glass rabbit statues from downstairs.

"What kind of task?" Seeing no other way out especially with his power blasting at me full force, I had to ask the question even if it irked me.

"I'm looking for an object." He sat on the edge of the desk, crossing one ankle over the other. "I was told you are very good at making objects disappear."

Fear jolted through me.

No one knew I took small things from the others in my clan. No one. But the knowing look on his face could not be faked, so I kept my mouth shut, my heart in my throat. Nigel flicked his gaze to my neck, which curdled my blood.

"I need you to find it and bring it to me." he said quietly still fascinated with the thrumming vain on the side of my neck.

"That's it?" Selina shifted behind me, reminding me she was still in the same spot I found her. "A magical object I presume?"

"Indeed."

"You are aware I need to know what it is so I can find it

and bring it to you, right?" All the short replies and questions were getting to me.

"I need a book. I'm sure you can find that, and the place I expect is protecting it will have no other books around it."

"If it does, do I fill up a bag or call a U-Haul?" Tired of his evasive answers, I rolled my shoulders. "I assume you planned to have me cornered like this and you had a hand in setting yourself up as my target tonight. Since there is no option for me to back down alive, let's hear it. I will not go into anything blind. Not anymore. Look where not having enough information got me."

"Touché." Unless I was losing my eyesight, I could've sworn I saw respect in the stormy gray of his irises. "The book I want is guarded in the mage's guild."

For the second time since I stepped into this room, numbness spread through me and a whooshing sound filled my ears. It took a long moment to unstick my tongue from the roof of my mouth so I could speak.

"Which book is it?" I really, truly didn't want to hear the answer.

"The Necronomicon."

"Mother fudge!" My knees wobbled as I spat the words.

Chapter Eight

Silence pressed heavily on my shoulders while Nigel and Selina watched me with unwavering focus. Not like I could see them doing it, but I could feel the weight of their stares on my skin, pulling it tighter than it needed to be. My unseeing eyes were clouded from long-ago-buried memories that I'd tried my best to forget. My mother's gentle smile as she ran her hand over my hair. Or my father's laughter when I tripped over my own feet and his kind eyes while he wiped the blood from my scraped hands or knees. The carefree childhood that was taken from me danced at the forefront of my mind, along with the one thing that made it happen.

Necronomicon.

I couldn't remember details clearly from that fateful day when my parents were killed, but I'll never forget the repeated whispering of that name. I'd heard many stories since then about the elusive book, none which were the truth. When it came to the mage's guild, you could say they loved making themselves sound mysterious and too powerful to be angered. Embellishing things was their forte, and making up stories about a simple book to justify all their atrocities would not surprise me at all.

But what if the stories were true?

What if the Necronomicon really was the Gate of the Gods? Every time I'd asked, people would nervously dart their eyes to make sure no one was around before warnings to never mention it again spilled from their lips in a rush. Master Bowmen even told me numerous times that if I valued my life, I'd never speak of it again.

It's what had your parents killed, nibbling. Don't ever mention that again," he'd told me with so much fear and sorrow on his wrinkled face that I eventually stopped asking. Now I, once again, had to face the cursed thing and I had no knowledge of anything that could help me get out of this disaster.

"You are thinking too hard, Ms. Jansen." Nigel's deep voice brought me out of the downward spiral my thoughts were taking. "As much as it pains me to send you to steal from your own, it must be done."

"You do look really pained." Rolling my eyes at the useless words he said just to fill the silence, I clenched and unclenched my fists to bring some circulation to my numbed fingers. "I need to hear everything you know about this Necronomicon if you want me to attempt to break into the mage's guild. If you know where you are sending me, I'm sure you are aware that a fate worse than death awaits me if I get caught."

"What makes you believe that, Ms. Jansen?" My words must've rubbed him wrong because his face darkened sending a shiver crawling up and down my spine. It centered at the base of my skull, throbbing in warning.

"The Magician loves spreading his stories for the rest of you to fear him, yet he can't even attempt to kill me without me knowing about it. I want the Necronomicon, and after you bring it to me, you will never see me again as long as you live. What do you think he can do to you that I cannot?"

Publicly killing me just like he did my parents while stealing their magic from their dying breaths lingered on my tongue, but I bit on it to keep my mouth shut. The face of the son-of-a-biscuit-eater floated in my mind, which clouded my logical thoughts. The five-year-old me who lost everything that day so long ago came to the surface, and the same fear crashed over me like a tidal wave.

Without thinking, magic burst from my fingertips. Deep red in color, menacing, and lethal, it curled up as if daring the vampire to come closer. The short swords I clutched tightly in my hands glinted icy blue amid all the fiery tendrils, and everything around me slowed to a crawl, each blink of the vampire's eyelashes measured as if lasting too long.

I could kill him.

I knew all I had to do was plunge both blades inside his chest while feeding them my magic and he would be no more. Darkness lurked at the back of my mind as if cheering me on and daring me to do it. I had to do everything I could to protect the Necronomicon and keep it out of his hands. Out of anyone's hands. No one could be allowed near it, at least not as long as I was alive.

Gasping from those thoughts, I stumbled backwards, my eyes widening as I dropped my swords, which disappeared before they even hit the carpeted floor. Nigel frowned, his concerned eyes watching me, but he was unaware how close he had been to death. With my hands trembling, I kept stepping back until the back of my knees hit the bed and I plopped on it heavily. The vampire was not helping me at all, his eyes staring into me as he cocked his head to the side, a thoughtful look plastered all over his face.

"I have no intention of harming you if you do what I've asked you to do," he tells me evenly, not a single muscle on his face twitching. It was almost like he didn't want to spook me.

A bark of humorless laughter passed through my tingling lips.

"Sorry to burst your bubble, Margie. Holding me here against my will and trying to blackmail me counts for intent to harm." If he noticed me wiping my sweaty palms off the bed sheets, he didn't show it. His gray irises were glued to my face as if he was searching for something.

"You did try to kill me, did you not Ms. Jansen?" Gliding closer to where I was sitting on the bed, he loomed over me, unintentionally spiking up the fear still lingering inside me. "Do tell me. If I was indeed asleep in my bed, would you have stabbed me in the back?"

"Yes." Just remembering that I really plunged my swords in the bundled-up pillows when I thought someone was sleeping under the covers had bile burning the back of my throat. A new wave of panic burst through me. I was going to murder in cold blood. I really would have killed someone by stabbing him in the back, not even giving him a chance to fight for his life.

I was as much of a monster as the rest of them.

"So how is what I'm doing any different?" Oblivious to my internal turmoil, Nigel kept talking. "At least I am looking you in the eye while offering you a chance to live. To save yourself. You, need I remind you, did not extend the same courtesy to me tonight."

"You are alive." My voice lacked the fire behind my words because I had no fight left inside of me.

"Not because of lack of effort on your part."" An arrogant smirk tilts one corner of his mouth up. "I must give credit where it's due. I've just gotten very good over the years at staying one step ahead of my enemies."

"Am I?" Irked by his cockiness, I scowled at him.

"Are you what, Ms. Jansen?"

The penetrating stare would be unnerving if he added a glimpse of his fangs, but thankfully he didn't. "You know that, for me, this was just a job. You are a target and simply a name. It's nothing personal."

"Are you what, Ms. Jansen?" Showing his stubborn side, he watched me unblinking.

"Your enemy," I blurted out.

"That all depends on what you decide tonight."

With a deep breath, my gaze darted around the hotel room, bouncing off the sparse furniture in it until it landed on Selina, who was still sitting on the windowsill with the elder wand casually resting between her fingers. Her upper body was leaning slightly forward, the eagerness to hear what I would say obvious in her body language. When she saw me staring at her, a goofy smile curled her lips and she shrugged as if unconcerned by my glare.

"If I agree to your threat"—My eyes find Nigel's again and I ignore the witch—"will I have all the information I need to get the book for you and leave the guild alive?"

"It would be poor judgment on my part to send you to take something I wanted if I didn't think you'd live long enough to bring it to me, don't you think?"

"You don't want to hear what I think right now, trust me." Acceptance that I had to do this because there was no other way out blanketed me like a cloak of doom. "Answer my question."

"You will have all the information you need to find the book and bring it to me, yes." It didn't escape me that he didn't actually answer my question. He would tell me only what I needed to know to get him the stupid book. For everything else, I'd be on my own.

"I bet Selina could fetch it even better than I could. Why not use the person you trust instead of blackmailing someone like me, who could run to The Magician and tell him your plans?" My smile grew, while his eyes turned into slits. "I'll bet my magic that he would love to hear all about it."

When he leaned forward and put us so close our faces are almost touching, my heart hammered my ribcage, then his nose grazed mine and I could feel his breath on my lips. The power wafting off him battered me like a ram. It switched the intensity as it glided over my skin like a gentle lover's caress. I stayed still, twisting my fingers in the bedsheets and grinding my teeth when my body reacted to him as he knew it would. That damn smirk lifting one side of his mouth told me he was well aware of everything. The scent of his skin mixed with the heavy smell of blooming roses brought a moment of weakness, but a crazy idea comes out of nowhere. Without thinking about it too much, I leaned forward and pressed my lips to his.

I never claimed to be smart all the time.

Nigel stilled, the breath hitching in his throat as his lips molded to mine. What was a split second in time lasts for an eternity. Both of us were caught off guard, him by my audacity and me by my own stupidity, until his hand wrapped around my hair and he tugged me closer, a low groan rumbling in his chest. The tip of his tongue grazed my lips asking for entrance, which snapped me out of my hormonal daze. I stiffened as I pushed away from him.

The hand holding my hair tightened painfully.

"Selina, out." Nigel's voice was barely above a whisper, while his gray eyes bore into mine as if he was trying to see my soul.

Fear jolted through my limbs as I tried to back away, but he tightened his hold on my hair, not releasing me from that intense gaze. From the corner of my eye I saw the outline of the witch moving, her fast obedience to his murmured order rustling the curtains with a soft breeze. The click of the door opening and gently closing was like a nail in my brain.

He didn't look away.

"It is a very dangerous game you are playing, Ms. Jansen." He yanked on my hair, tugging my feet when I tried to duck to escape his knowing eyes. "So young, yet so much power. You hide it so well that nobody would even guess it was in there. Well, unless you slip like you did a few minutes ago. Who taught you to ward it like that?"

"I have no idea what you are talking about?" Embarrassed and angry, I placed both hands on his chest, hoping to shove him away. He didn't move an inch.

"Why didn't you kill me when you had a chance?" Long, thick lashes lower over his gray irises, and then the vampire cocked his head to the side.

Distrust was plastered all over his handsome face, and I knew one wrong word from me could set him off. If that happened, he'd rip my jugular before I could even blink. Danger covered him like a cloak as he stood unnaturally motionless. He wasn't even blinking to make it seem like he had any human qualities. No, Nigel Toucher was all predator, and he was solely focused on his prey at the moment. And the worst of all, he was actually acutely aware of my magic acting up earlier when I naively believed he'd missed the whole thing. The reality of my situation hit me like a harsh slap to the face.

This time I bit off more than I could chew.

"I'm not warding anything." Shoulders dropping in defeat, I sagged in his hold, although it hurt like a mother trucker when strands of my hair rip from my scalp. "My magic is unpredictable."

"Unpredictable how?" Taken aback by my honesty, he untangled his fingers from my hair, one single strand remaining in his hand. He brought it under his nose and sniffed. "You have clan magic. All of you have unpredictable powers, which is what makes you so dangerous—and a worthy adversary."

"Right." Snorting without humor, I plopped back on the bed and scrubbed a hand over my face. "Mine comes and goes as it pleases, in case you didn't notice. I knew this was a trap when they sent me after you."

"Not unpredictable." The mattress dipped when he sat next to me, making my body shift closer to his. "Unstable, then."

"What?" The vampire's nearness made my mind turn into a scrambled mess, so I gawk at him as if he'd just spoken in tongues.

"And they didn't send you into a trap." Giving me a side-eyed glance, he bumped his shoulder on mine. "I made sure it was you who was given the target."

"So you could blackmail me into stealing for you?" I accuse him flatly. "How on earth did you trick The Magician into doing what you wanted?"

"A bloke can't tell you all his secrets, Ms. Jansen." Chuckling, Nigel turned to face me and the boyish grin on his face made my heart skip a beat. "I have a feeling

I'll have to reveal those very slowly to keep your attention."

"If I'm still alive by the morning," I point out the anvil hanging around my neck. "When he realizes you are not dead, The Magician is coming after me."

"Who said he won't be told that I'm dead in the morning?" The room spun around me from the implications in his softly spoken words.

Chapter Nine

When one agreed to make a deal with the devil himself, one had a moment of clarity. And right that very minute, it was trying to choke me. With a tight throat, I stared at the opposite wall because I couldn't form a coherent thought. No, I had just enough energy left in me to breathe. And blink.

Nigel, after dropping that little bomb and announcing his plan to fool The Magician into thinking that my mission was actually successful, got on his phone, his words shooting from his mouth in a language I didn't understand. It sounded old, and I wondered how his tongue didn't break while trying to pronounce some of the longer words. Crazy, I knew, but all I had left right then was that: listening to the vampire speak and breathe without understanding a word he said.

Breathing is nice, I reminded myself.

Stuck in the dumb hotel room for some ridiculous reason, I was a little too aware of the glass rabbits sprinkled in the lobby and all around the ground floor. I rubbed my unevenly cut nail over the smooth sheets on the bed, letting it catch the soft fibers until it pulled them out of the thread. If I didn't keep my hands occupied, magic flew from my fingers in short bursts like I was spitting fireworks.

Not something I wanted the vampire to see.

The cloying scent of the vase, which was full of blooming white roses, filled my nostrils until the back of my throat tingled. I wasn't sure if that was how those particular roses smelled or if Selina had something to do with the overwhelming scent. I wouldn't put it past her to do something like that just to make my life miserable. I saw a reoccurring theme between her and Nigel. Since I couldn't make either of them as frustrated as I was, I glared at the flowers as if it was their fault the night had gone south and to smithereens.

"Ms. Jansen?" Nigel yanked me out of my thoughts, a frown puckering his forehead like he'd been calling my name for a while.

"Gee, bloodsucker, give a girl a break, would you?" Pressing my palm to the center of my chest, I tried to calm the wild beating of my heart. "Weren't you just billy bopping with tongue twisters a second ago on your phone?" Shooing him off with a flick of my wrist, I ignored the frustrated glare he sent my way. "Go do your thing. Make yourself deader than a door nail. It'll keep both of us alive a little longer."

"You truly are more afraid of him than you are me." His eyebrows crawled up his forehead until they almost disappeared under the lock of hair falling over one of his eye. I watch in fascination as his hand smoothed it back, tightening the hem of his sleeve around his arm.

A rap on the door stiffened my spine.

"Bugger off." His British accent comes out loud and clear. It reminded me of who he was, but also that we were not hanging around this stupid hotel because we had nothing better to do. The dimwit took me hostage so I could do his bidding.

"Fiddlesticks. And you frown at *my* cussing." Mouth twisted in distaste, I rolled my eyes when he narrowed his gaze on me. "Bugger off." Butchering the crap out of his accent, I mimicked his deep voice.

"I don't think that fiddlesticks is even a swear word ..."

"I don't care." Pronouncing each word slowly, I jutted my chin up.

"In a few minutes The Magician will be notified of my death." Choosing to be the bigger person and ignore my childish behavior, he stretched both his arms over his head. "That means you will need to return to your clan and sell the lie, Ms. Jansen."

"What?" I squeaked. "You've lost your marbles. Have you met me?" Gaping at him incredulously, I couldn't believe my eyes when he grinned at me like a fool. "I can't lie!" Jumping on my feet, I paced in front of him. "Might as well just kill me now. No one will even blame you for it, really. I knew this was a bad idea. I should've just pissed Selina off so she could zap me with the elder wood wand. At least it would've been a worthy death."

"Ms. Jansen—"

"Don't you 'Ms. Jansen' me you son of a cracked nut!" Nigel's eyes widened when I whirled on him. "My uncle will know I'm actually thinking of lying before he even sets his eyes on me. I'm going to die for lying. Not for some glorious misfortune while hunting a target, or even for chasing an informant through this damn city. No, I'll lose my life for being unable to lie. That's more embarrassing than being flogged in the middle of the mage's guild for attempting to steal a book from them, one that no one has ever seen. I'll bet my magic that it doesn't even exist. There you have it! I'll die for a myth."

"Charlie." My name on those lips closed my mouth with a snap. It was that damn accent of his. I stared at him owlishly.

He opened his mouth to speak again, but my brain caught up to what he said and I beat him to it. "You are letting me go?"

"Our little deception won't work if you don't show up to confirm that the target has been eliminated."

"Exactly." My cheeks hurt when a smile stretched across my face. "So, I'll be on my way then, and you just stay here and wait this out." Spinning on my heel, I head for the door with an urgency I'd never felt before. "And don't worry. I'm going to lie out of my ears if I have to, selling your corpse like it's the hottest thing on the market. Martha Stewart has nothing on me, you just wait."

My boot catches on the thick carpet, the move pitching my body forward until I smack the vase full of flowers in my haste to stop myself. The air hitched in my throat, both my arms shooting out in a fruitless attempt to keep me standing. A split second of panic sent numbness racing over my body, and the next thing I knew, my face was close enough to the ground that I could count the fibers on the plush carpet. Squeezing my eyes shut, I braced for the impact and prayed that my nose wouldn't break. That would hurt like a mother trucker, but it might help me sell the lie that I killed the bloodsucker. All that goes through my mind in that tiny moment of time before pain would explode in my skull.

Wind whooshed in my ears, and a sharp pain zinged from my neck across my shoulders. The back of my head landed softly on a cushioned palm. The dull thump of something heavy hitting the carpeted floor penetrated the sound of rushing blood in my ears from somewhere in the room. Too afraid to open my eyes in case I was still going to slam face first into the ground, I pried one eyelid open tentatively. Nigel's blurry face danced in front of me, but it was much too close for comfort. The vampire didn't just catch me before I hit the ground, he managed to flip me over so that my back was barely touching the floor. It should scare the hell out of me that he could move so fast, but it was oddly comforting.

"I think I need glasses." My voice sounded squeaky and panicked.

"Try opening both your eyes, Ms. Jansen." Ignoring the barely suppressed humor in his words, I did just that, blinking rapidly to clear my vision.

"Right. No glasses needed."

Too aware of how close his face was to mine, I turned to the side and looked past his shoulders. The colorful vase was on the floor, the white roses sprinkled around it. The water from inside was soaking into the carpet, and I watch the fabric darkening like it was the most interesting thing in the world.

"I better get going. The sooner I get back to my clan, the sooner I can lie my butt off and sell your death." Unwilling to look at him, I squirmed so he would move away.

He didn't.

Clearing my throat, I pushed at him timidly with both hands to get him moving, but I get no results. Seeing no other option, my gaze flicked to his face and my stomach tightened from the look in his gray eyes. Something lurked in those irises, old and calculating. It sends alarms blaring in my head.

"Not so fast, Ms. Jansen," Nigel murmurs, his eyes

darting to my lips before locking on mine again. My mouth was too dry when I tried to swallow. "I need some assurance that you will be back here tomorrow night."

"You have my word. There you go, now get off me." I almost headbutted him when I tried to get up, but he stayed unmoving like a statue.

A dark chuckle rumbled in his chest.

"I'm happy to take your word, but I will need something more than that I'm afraid." Icicles spread through my veins when his gaze zeroed in on my neck.

"What do you need?" Proud that my voice didn't waiver, I held my breath, hoping beyond hope that I was wrong.

"I will need your blood."

He wasn't even done talking when my magic burst out of me in a wave strong enough to throw him across the room. Barely missing the windows, Nigel hit the wall so hard the glass rattled and cracks spread like spiderwebs all over the nicely painted room. Plaster and dust rained over him turning his hair ashen after he dropped on his knees, his head bowed like he was in prayer. All the dirt covering him turned him into the statue he closely resembled when he stood unnaturally still, which only reminded me that he was on the top of the food chain in my world.

Scrambling to get up and with every intention of running out of there as fast as my feet would carry me, I froze when Nigel lifted his head, his gray eyes glowing dimly on the dirt-covered face. The smile curling his mouth chills my blood, and when the tips of his fangs poked from under his upper lip, my heart dropped between my feet.

Spinning around too fast to keep my balance, I hit my shoulder off the corner of the wall as I head toward the hallway. The door was close but still too far for me to reach as the short hairs at the back of my neck stand on end from the nearness of the predator at my back. I knew he was not on me yet, but I felt the warmth of his body searing my skin. With only one goal at the center of my mind, my hand reached for the doorknob, and I grazed the cold metal with the tips of my fingers.

A hand twisted the back of my shirt, jerking me back and flinging my body to the center of the room. My back hit the floor hard enough that not even the thick carpet could stop the air punching out of my lungs. Gasping and coughing, I scissored my legs, flipping around and landing in a crouch with one hand pressed on the carpet between my knees so I didn't end up on my butt. Wild strands of hair fell over my face, and between them I saw the vampire prowling toward me.

"I need just a drop to keep track of you, Ms. Jansen. I won't harm you." His voice sounded much deeper than before, the words slurred slightly through the vicious fangs protruding from his gums.

"I wasn't born yesterday, you dumbnut." Hissing the words with great effort from my starving lungs, I flicked the hand not supporting my weight calling out my sword to manifest. "Many of your kind have tried to take blood from an assassin mage, and none have been successful to this day for a reason. You will get nowhere near my blood while I'm still alive."

"I do not want your magic. I just need a drop to be sure that you will not run." Keeping an eye on my blade, he inched cautiously forward, very unlike the earlier confident prowl he had.

"If you want blood"—Getting to my feet so I didn't have him looming over me, I pushed the hair out of my face—"you'll have to draw it first. You will not get it willingly."

His nostrils flared and I clenched my hand not holding a

sword into a fist. When he threw me back, I rolled over the stupid roses and the thorns ripped my palm open deep enough that the warm trickle on my skin didn't go unnoticed. With a cocky grin, I sent my magic to my palm, healing it as I wiped it off my pants in slow, purposeful movements.

A muscle jumped on one side of his jaw.

"I don't think this arrangement will work." Releasing the second sword, I twirled both between my fingers. I might be many things, but idiotic I was not. One sip of my blood would make an unstoppable vampire strong enough to destroy the whole city in one night. I would not be responsible for that many lives. Not if I could help it.

"You cannot believe I need your help, or anyone's for that matter. If I wanted to rampage through this city and bathe it in blood, Ms. Jansen, I would." Ducking his head to bring us eye level, he watched me through his lashes. "You haven't done your homework correctly if that's what you think."

"You need help to get that book." Pointing one of the swords at his chest, I let my magic curl around it, the deep red tendrils coiling like a snake and nipping at him in the air. "The stories you tell don't match."

"I need your help so that no one has to die." Straightening his shoulders, Nigel stretched to his full height. "But you are correct." At my confusion, he offered a reassuring smile, which only made me more suspicious. "I have other ways to track you, a drop of blood was just easier and less expensive. I'll abide by your wishes. You are free to go."

Not trusting him a bit, I didn't move. He stood with both arms hanging loosely at his sides, relaxed like we didn't just try to kill each other. When long moments passed and nothing changed, I inched around him, giving the bloodsucker a wide girth. Those gray eyes tracked my every move, but he didn't attack. A small smile played on his lips, and it was unnerving me enough to speed up my exit.

With my heart punching like a war drum in my chest and a tight hold on my swords, I reached the door, and with very little fumbling I fling it open. Nigel didn't attack, following at my back from a safe distance. Unsure if it was because he really was telling the truth or he was worried I'd flip around and plunge the swords between his ribs, I locked my eyes on the elevator down the hall and headed toward it with purpose.

No one met me in the hallway as my boots silently crushed the thick carpet. This hotel was made for assassinations, so it was easy to move around without being heard. Something I should point out to Master Bowmen when I got home. That thought urged my feet to move faster, and as soon I reached the button, I pressed the button hard enough I almost broke the damn thing.

"Don't forget to be back here tomorrow night, Ms. Jansen," Nigel drawled from behind me. "I'd hate to come looking for you in your home."

I'm sure they'll be happy to see you there, is what I'm thinking. "I will be back," is what I told the bloodsucker.

The elevator pinged before the doors start sliding open. I sucked in a harsh breath when Nigel took a fistful of my hair, spinning me around and crushing his mouth on mine. His tongue dove between my lips, tangling and gliding around mine. My brain scrambled, erasing all reasons why this was a bad idea. His scent overwhelmed me, his taste overriding all rational thought. A moan was wrenched from deep in my chest. He tightened his hold until all I knew were his lips and hands. I chased him when he buried his face in my hair, his hot breath raising goosebumps over my legs and arms when it puffed on my ear.

"You should've killed me when you had the chance, Ms. Jansen." His breathless, raspy words took a moment to register in my muddled brain.

Something soft brushed my skin where my neck met my shoulder right before a sharp pinch jolted me out of the daze. His warm, wet tongue licked all the way to the back of my ear just as the warmth of my blood wetted my skin. With a hard push he sent me stumbling inside the elevator, and my shocked eyes locked on the white rose he was holding in his hand. The large thorn at the top was covered in my blood, and so was the bottom of the soft petals. An arrogant smirk danced on Nigel's lips.

"You are fighting this attraction a little too hard, Ms. Jansen." The doors started sliding closed, and when I could barely see him between the gap, he threw the rose at my chest. It hit the floor between my feet while I watched his face disappear. "Don't be late tomorrow night." His voice came from behind the closed door as I descended to the ground floor.

"What have I done?" The words were just a breath passing my numb lips.

Chapter Ten

The chilly night air brushed against my skin as I walked out in a daze through the front doors of the hotel. The sting of the thorn lingered on my neck like a ghost pain, reminding me that things couldn't get worse tonight if The Magician himself stood in front of me threatening my life. It was all fun and games, and everything could be forgiven—even a klutz like me who had no control of her magic whatsoever. At least until a line no one had dared cross was crossed. Our magic was only good as long as we were still breathing. Those born like me had taken their own lives to prevent anyone from having their blood.

Tripping on the last step, I stumbled down the sidewalk with wobbling knees. The dread eating thought my stomach like acid numbed me from any embarrassment I would've felt. Why did it matter if anyone knew I could barely walk a straight line when I might've just doomed us all? Were a few drops enough to double Nigel's powers? Would it give him additional strengths that no one was aware off? Did it even matter at all?

I almost jumped out of my skin when a horn blared loudly, the lights from the car blinding me as it veered off to speed around my dumb butt. Lost in my thoughts, I'd walked out to the middle of the street without checking for traffic. Dragging my feet that weigh a ton, I couldn't find it in me to care if I was run over. It would be a better death than knowing I was assassinated for betraying everyone. Reaching the scooter, I plopped on it, wobbling the rusty crotch rocket and almost ending up with it crushing my legs. It was a good thing it was the middle of the night so no one saw me wrestling with the handles as my heart jumped to my throat. When I finally had it under control, I slung my leg over it and looked across the street at the many dark windows of the hotel rooms. A few of them had the light on, but only one had the curtains pulled apart and a figure standing in it looking down. I didn't need to see that far to know it was the vampire. He was probably gloating at his victories, while I debated if staying alive was worth it.

To make matters worse, butterflies erupted in my lower belly as a flashback of our kiss and his taste came uninvited to my tongue. If I didn't know better I'd say it was one of his powers: to make anyone remember whatever he wanted them to, even from afar. Was that a thing?

When it came to Nigel Thatcher, anything was possible.

Dragging my eyes away from the mother trucker, I mashed the start button hard enough to get it stuck in its frame. The scooter spat and stuttered, the muffler coughing out clouds of black smoke behind me before it died with a pathetic wailing sound. Muttering words that made my ears burn under my breath, I picked at the button with my nail, hoping to pop it out so I could try again. Get the old thing moving to go ... where exactly?

The Magician

Knowing what I had to do and doing it were two different things. The gloomy thoughts clouding my mind were not helping me make the right decisions, and I knew as well as I knew my own name that my uncle would be able to tell something was off the second he saw me. One thing going for the vampire at the moment was that I had a bigger lie to sell than his death.

A vampire took my blood.

Jabbing rapidly at the start button on the scooter, I finally got it started, the sound of the motor filling the deserted street like the scene of a world war two movie, *rat-tat-tat-ing* loud enough to raise the dead. Preferring to wander around the city on foot, I never found it necessary to get a car. A decision I was reminded of after every ride by my rat's-nest hair, and one I regretted greatly tonight.

The salty tang in the air stung my nostrils as I sped down the street, my arms trembling with each turn because I gripped the handles a tad too tight. I might've called it a speed off, but that was a bit of a stretch. It was more like my scooter jerking in stutters down the road before it picked up speed and dropped to a crawl. The wind pelted my skin, but my cold, sweat-drenched skin had my shirt sticking to my stomach, chest and back. Buildings blurred into distant shapes looming around me. When I finally stopped, I had to blink rapidly to clear my vision, and I thanked whoever was watching over me for not letting me get killed because of the roads I'd taken. I didn't remember how I got to the dark parking lot I found myself in.

Smoothing the crazy strands of hair sticking out in every direction around my head, I stared at the Victorian-style building, the balconies curling around it like small smiley faces gracing the passersby. Peeked roof towers on two sides reached for the dark sky, the arched windows facing the street like two glaring eyes pinning me to my spot. It could be my imagination, but I got the feeling the building itself was warning me to stay away from it and the person living inside in one of the apartments. Too bad I was past the point of making the morally correct decisions tonight.

Feeling like I was older than dirt, I forced my feet to move and I climbed the stairs to the second floor, passing the ornament vases stuffed with fake flowers in the narrow hallway to reach the door at the end. Standing there for what felt like forever as I held my breath with my knuckles raised, I finally rapped on the wooden door much louder than I expected. Wincing, I glanced over my shoulder, expecting someone to pop their head out from the other two apartments and put me in my place. When forcefully woken from their sleep, humans seemed very brave I'd noticed.

I shouldn't have come here.

Panic made me spin on my heels, and my shoulders slightly hunched in my attempt to bolt and disappear, but the soft crack of the door opening behind me stops me mid-turn.

"Charlie?" Tia's soft voice was raspy from sleep, and my throat tightened from guilt because I woke her up. "Charlie, what are you doing here in the middle of the night?" When I didn't respond fast enough for her, she huffs in frustration, so I turn to face her.

My friend's normally immaculate appearance was nowhere to be found. The blonde strands that never had a hair out of place were bundled in a messy bun atop her head, and it looked like it had tilted sideways in her sleep. Now, what seemed like a pulled wool ball stuck out just above her right ear as she squinted at me through racoon eyes where the mascara hadn't washed off and had smudged under her eyes. The pink tank top and shorts she wore were twisted around her petite frame as she shuffled her bare feet forward to lean on the doorframe and give me a better look. I'd never dare remind her of what I saw when she drilled me about looking more like a woman instead of a homeless person.

"Were you sleeping?" Even I could tell the smile I gave her was strained and visibly forced.

"Isn't that what normal people do at four in the morning?" Tucking her chin to her chest, she watched me like I'd lost my mind.

"You are not normal." Not knowing what else to say, I repeated something she loved reminding everyone: that she wasn't normal or like other people.

"I have trained you well Padawan." Grinning like a fool, she waved me in, but I stood rooted in the hallway. "Charlie, get your ass inside so the neighbors don't come out and see me half naked."

"You are more covered now than when you are dressed." That was a bad thing to say. Not something you pointed out when Tia was half awake, I learned.

"Seriously?" Wide awake now, she glared at me, her blue eyes glinting as sharp as my blades. "You came here in the middle of the night to lecture me about modesty? How very nice of you."

Mouth pressed in a thin line, the run-down mascara blackening her pale skin, she did look like a rabid racoon when she took a step out the door, her messy bun bouncing above her ear in irritation. She grabbed my arm and yanked me inside her apartment in a swift move. Stumbling and hitting my elbow on the wall in the small entrance area, I rubbed at it while I gave her the stink eye. Staring back, she purposely closed the door slowly behind her as if daring me to say something. If I wasn't one-hundred percent sure that she was human, I would've sworn she'd grow claws and sharp teeth and rip me apart.

"What happened?" Folding her arms across her chest, she waited for an answer, one of her feet tapping impatiently on the floor.

"Who says something happened?" Wincing at how defensive I sounded, I blew out a breath through pursed lips. "I was bored, couldn't sleep, and didn't think of what time it was before I came here. Sorry ..." Adding the last part lamely, it was me who shuffled uncomfortably.

"Right." Sighing, she looked at me with worry shining in her eyes, and I had to swallow the lump trying to choke me. "Let's go sit down so you can tell me why you couldn't sleep."

I allowed Tia to guide to her living room with one hand on my arm. Her home was just like her personality: all bold colors and in-your-face sharp lines daring you to challenge her presence in this world. Deep green walls with golden metallic accents made the bright red couch and two armchairs stand out like sore thumbs in the space, with snow white tiles covering the floor. White, black, and bright yellow pillows were thrown haphazardly on the furniture, one ending up on the round coffee table, the glass top propped on the tail and shoulder of a stone mermaid. Sheer yellow curtains rustled on each side of the open window, the breeze cooling the temperature of the room to a barely comfortable level. Fairy lights were strung around abstract paintings of blues and purples all over the walls. The black flat-screen TV looked out of place, a touch of modern technology in a room where a unicorn got sick and had a rainbow diarrhea.

"I killed someone tonight." The words spilled out with no infliction. I didn't really kill anyone, but I did have to make it believable if my clan was to live. Plus, I could've killed him if the vampire hadn't been too smart for my own good.

You could hear a pin drop.

"Say what now?" Tia nudged me to her couch and pushed me down until my butt molded to whatever foam the thing was made from. "Actually, hold that thought." Her forefinger stuck out in front of her face and she took a deep breath. "I need a drink first, and you do too by the sound of it." Muttering something else under her nose that sounded suspiciously like she was telling herself to wake up because it was just another one of those dreams, she rushed to the kitchen.

I wiped my sweaty palm off her silly couch before taking the glass she handed me, while she was gulping whatever she poured into hers. Staring at the liquid while she disappeared again, she returned with a freshly filled glass. I keep wondering why I came here. The strong scent of alcohol slapping me in the face made my eyes water, and I touched it to my lips without drinking so I didn't offend her. Tia raised her eyebrow and perched on the armrest, which told me I hadn't fooled her like I'd hoped.

"Let's try again." Twirling her wrist, she watched my face intently. If I wasn't so messed up right now, I would've laughed at how ridiculous she looked.

"I killed someone tonight." I glued my eyes to the glass in my hand like it was my precious just so I didn't look at her. Repeating it enough times would make me believe it, right?

"Who did you kill and what did they do?" Her penetrating stare was drilling holes in the side of my face, and I couldn't help but squirm. "I know you Charlie, and you wouldn't hurt a fly if you could help it. If you killed someone, they deserved it. What did they do?"

I said nothing.

The words died on my tongue and guilt crippled me. I shouldn't have come here. I shouldn't be lying to her. And I had to go back to the place I called home and continue to lie even more before leaving to enter the mage's guild. Then I have to attempt to steal a book no one had ever seen. All because I was useless as an assassin and they used me against my clan. All so me and mine could live.

"Okay." I startled when Tia jumped on her feet. "Okay, we got this."

"What?" Gaping at her in confusion, I watched as she yanked the elastic holding the fluffed-up ball of hair to the side of her head.

"We got this." Strands of hair fell on the floor when she tugged her fingers through it in her attempt to brush it out. "This is why I buy stupid shit. I like to be prepared, but this caught me off guard."

"What are you talking about?" Blinking like a dummy, I found it hard to pick my jaw off the floor. "What?"

"I don't have shovels." My friend looked angry at that, and I was more confused than ever. "But!" Her forefinger goes up again. "I'm sure someone has one in the garage, right? It's Virginia after all. We have snow, Charlie."

"You are not making any sense, Tia."

"I don't need to make sense, I have a plan. After we fix this you will tell me all about it, even if I have to beat it out of you. I'm not joking." Still in her tank top and shorts, she moved for the door. "I hope you remember where you left the body because that part is very important, so think hard if you have to. I might actually kill them too, although they are already dead so it won't make much difference. Wait here, I'll be right back." Throwing the words over her shoulder, she was out the door before I could stop her.

Chapter Eleven

Hell had no fury like my human friend on a mission to save me from going to jail. Returning from her trip to the garage, which was located on the ground level of the building where the resident had more junk they didn't use than actual cars, Tia opened the door with her elbow and kicked it closed with her foot. In her right hand she triumphantly held a snow shovel as if she was Poseidon walking in brandishing his trident. A large bundle of what looked like an old tent was tucked under the armpit of the other arm while she stood facing me with a large grin on her face, though I thought it looked a bit feral. Add to that the black mascara under her eyes and she appeared more like a feral panda ready to do some Kung Fu.

"I told you. Snow." Waving the snow shovel, she almost broke the ornate mirror hanging on the wall above the skinny end table in the small entrance.

This was one of the main reasons I liked Tia in the first place. She was all fun and games until the moment she thought you need help. Be it how to dress like a woman—

which she called fashion police—or hiding an imaginary body in a case like tonight. Loyalty was something my friend took seriously. She would go down like a captain with his ship for those she called her own. Something I should learn from her since by letting her come here I'd placed her life in danger.

Barking out a humorless laugh, I groaned as I scrubbed a hand over my face. There was nothing funny about the situation, but I finally got the clarity of why I'd come to Tia instead of to my clan where I belonged. There was a need pulsing inside of me to tell someone everything, all of it, and it was too strong to ignore. And the sad part was that apart from Tia, I didn't trust another person to bare my soul to. Not even my uncle.

"You are in shock." Misinterpreting my slumped shoulders and barely held back tears, she dropped everything with a clank and rushed to my side. "It's okay girl, we will fix this. I'll chew through a carcass if I have to, but no one will find out. You just calm down and tell me where the body is."

One treacherous tear rolled down my cheek.

Tia's face blanched as if she'd seen a ghost.

I never cried.

"There is no body." My voice cracked at the end, so I had to clear my throat.

"Of course there is a body. It's what living beings walk this world with. Just remember where you left it and we are set." Smoothing the hair out of my face, she looked up at me from her crouch at my feet. With a reassuring squeeze to my knees, she mumbled under her breath what sounded like, "After that, I'm going to drink that whole bottle of tequila when I get back and pretend it was all a bad dream."

Shaking off the thought because I was sure I'd heard her wrong, I blew out a breath and made probably the worst decision in my entire life. "I lied." When her eyebrows dropped in confusion, I steeled my spine. "I didn't kill anyone, and that's not the only thing I've lied to you about."

"Okaaayyy." Lowering her butt on the white tiles, she folded her legs underneath her and gave me an expectant stare. "I'm not going to lie, I feel lost."

My mouth opened and words spilled out like a waterfall. I told her everything, from what I was, to what kinds of creatures shared the world with her. I was pretty sure it all came out jumbled in one breath because I had to a pause to suck in a lungful of air before continuing the word vomit that ended with my arrival at her door tonight.

I hoped she would hear me out, tell me I was crazy, and either call the cops to lock me up or a mental institution to pick me up. Anything would've sat better with me than the too-sharp stare focused on me at the moment. She didn't even blink, and her blue irises seemed like they could see and hear my thoughts. It was more unsettling than the fact that a vampire had taken my blood, which said a lot.

"I have a million questions right now, and I understand that lives are at stake here, but ..." Chewing on her bottom lip, I watched her internal battle until those blue orbs flicked to mine. "Show me."

"Huh?"

"You said you are a mage with magic." A nervous giggle came out of her. "Show me this magic. Can I see it, or do I have to imagine it's there?"

"You don't believe me."

"Actually, I must be as nuts as you because this is one thing that makes sense about you, Charlie. I just want to see

... please." Tia was all calm and collected, but I didn't miss the hard swallow she tried to hide.

Searching her eyes for a long moment, I slowly lifted my hand between us and didn't look away. Uncurling my fingers, I let a small trickle of my magic come to the surface, my palm tingling like it always did when the power lingered just underneath my skin. Red and blue tendrils unfolded, flickering between us and bathing her face in color. With great reluctance, she dragged her gaze away from mine and focused on it, her eyes widening slightly at the sight.

"Can I ..." Reaching with her hand, she stopped before making contact with the swirling magic. Morbid fascination was plastered over her features. "Can I touch it? It won't hurt me, right?"

"Not this little of it, no. It'll sting, though, so I don't think you should." When I tried to pull my hand away, she snatched my wrist and held me still. 'Tia." Saying her name in a warning didn't do squat.

"Oh, ye of little faith." Before I pulled the magic back, she placed her hand over mine, wincing at the sparks when it touched her skin. She didn't jerk away, though.

"Mother fudge." Yanking my hand out of her reach, I glared at her. "What is the matter with you? Which part of assassin mage clan didn't you understand?"

Tia ignored my outburst, staring at her now blistering palm like it was a bug under a microscope. I didn't know it'd burn her that badly. I'd never used it on a human before. Bile burned the back of my throat and my head swiveled around to look for something to help her. Seeing my still-full glass, I snatched it off the coffee table, and in my panic I dumped the alcohol over her burned hand. That got me the reaction I'd expected to begin with.

"Oh you fucker of all fucks!" Squealing, she jumped to

her feet while performing some tribal rain summoning dance. Just the firepit was missing, which she made up for by spitting flames through her eyes. That was what it looked like to me anyway. "What the hell did you do that for?" Flapping her hand frantically in front of her, she stomped in place while clenching her teeth.

"I told you not to touch it, so you burned yourself. What was I supposed to do?"

"Not dump tequila on it, dambass." The flapping of her hand sped up as she hissed at me. "It burns, it burns ... aarrrgghhhh."

Wanting to do something to help, her I jumped on my feet too, kicking the glass I left on the floor. It rolled toward Tia just as she brought one leg down and stomped, so of course it swept her feet out from under her. Eyes bugging out, we locked gazes and she hit the floor with a grunt, taking me with her. Ending in a pile of limbs was not what I had in mind when I told her everything.

"I think they somehow misplaced you." The words came out in a groan when my friend wiggled away from me. "Where I come from, assassin means a stealthy silent killer no one sees coming. You Charlie, with all due respect, are like an elephant in a china shop." Getting on her knees, she glanced down at me through wild hair. "Did they meet you before placing you in the clan or is it like a blind draw type a thing?"

"We are born like this." Snapping at her was not called for. She did have a point, but her comment hit too close to what I'd been hearing my entire life. "No one asked me what I wanted to be."

"And let me guess." Grabbing my forearm, she tugged me to stand up, keeping her burned hand away from both of us. "You would've rather been human, right?"

"Maybe." Unwilling to do psychoanalyses on myself at the moment, I begrudgingly let her comment slip, and allowed her to help me off the floor. "Listen, I trusted you with all this and I would like to think you'd keep my secret. No one is allowed to know that you know the truth. Do you understand?"

"Yeah, yeah." Waving my worry away, she plopped on the couch and huffed in annoyance. "If I say a word, they'll find me and remove the problem that could expose them. I've watched enough spy movies to know that."

"This is not a movie."

"Isn't it wonderful?" Grinning from ear to ear and all pain forgotten, I watched dumbfounded as her eyes sparkled in excitement. "I always knew there was something special about you."

"You mean apart from me being so graceful?"

"You being a klutz is just part of your charm, girl." Petting the couch, she waited until I gingerly sat next to her to continue. "All joking aside, tell me about this vampire. How can we outsmart him to get you out of his clutches."

"There is no we, Tia. It's *me*, and I'll deal with it. I just needed to get everything off my chest first, I guess. Like a last confession ... sort of."

"First of all, there is very much a *we*. Unless you want to test my stalking skills and determination, I suggest you count me in whatever you are planning." Her forefinger flicked up to silence my rebuttal. "Don't argue with me because you won't win. Second, is there a way I can get magic somehow?"

"Why in the fates name would you want that? Didn't you hear everything I just said?"

"If I hang around you more, maybe I'll learn?" Ignoring me like I hadn't spoken, she blinked innocently.

"Magic is not a disease and you can't catch it."

"Not a problem." Shrugging a shoulder, Tia was not deterred one bit. "Every sidekick is magicless and unassuming, but they are always the most important one in all stories."

"This is real life and you are not a sidekick." Scowling at her only broadened her smile. "I don't need a sidekick. I need to fix the mess I made."

"The best sidekick in the world coming to the rescue." Wiggling on the couch to get more comfortable she turned to face me better. "We will take everything one step at a time. Starting with teaching you how to lie with conviction."

Snorting a laugh, I shook my head at her. "Good luck with that." With a pathetic groan, I buried my face in the palms of my hands. "Fiddlesticks. What a mess."

"Second, we might teach you how to properly swear because, in all honesty, it's very pathetic." When I spread my fingers so I could see her through them, she huffed in indignation. "You are an assassin mage for God's sake, act like it. Don't worry, I got this."

"I'm not a project and there is nothing wrong with my choice of words."

"Of course not, honey." I'd never heard a more patronizing tone come out of Tia until that very moment. "We will work on that later. More important things need our attention now."

"Why do I get the feeling my life has gotten more complicated, and bear in mind I just got away from the most powerful vampire in the world?"

"Don't be silly. Two heads think better than one, that's all. Plus, I do make a hot sidekick." Giggling, she was getting a bit obsessive about this sidekick thing. "Unless the vamp was hot. Was he? Oh-em-gee, was he hot like in the romance novels? In that case, he will need gentle handling."

"Will you stop?" The anger in my voice had more to do with some stupid territorial feeling rearing its head when she mentioned Nigel than anything else she was saying.

I snapped my mouth shut.

"Got it." Mimicking zipping her lips, she turned her fingers as if she was locking it and pretending to throw the key. "No talking about fang boy. Understood. Let's work on the immediate problem first." At my raised eyebrow, her lips twisted into a grimace. "Go ahead, tell me you killed him. You did a great job when you walked in here tonight. I seriously believed you." To emphasize that truth, she looked pointedly at the tent and snow shovel still tossed on the ground.

"You are one thing. How in the world will I convince my uncle?" The sigh passing my lips came all the way from my toes.

"Easy." When my head snapped up to stare at Tia, she offered me a confident smile. "Practice. That's how you'll convince him you are telling the truth."

Chapter Twelve

I left Tia still muttering about sidekicks and learning magic while she helped me fight off the hottest male in existence, and found myself standing across the street from my home. My friend wasn't wrong about one thing: the vampire sure was very easy on the eyes. One more thing he used to get what he wanted, no doubt. Still, that wasn't why I was hesitating to walk up those steps and enter the mansion. No, I could feel someone watching, the uneasy prickling at the back of my neck warning me of danger.

Eyes darting around, I searched the area looking for something, anything to tell me where the sun of a gun was hiding. I would've been worried if I felt it around Tia's apartment, but luckily the prickling of eyes on me manifested when I came here. It was going to be a waiting game and whoever held out the longest between us would win. I had no intention on moving away from the cover of the thick tree and vehicles parked on the side of the road.

Flicking the collar of my jacket up to ward off the chill, I huddled closer to the trunk of the tree, blending in the shadows. My palms were itching to fling magic at the dumbnut until I hit him and force him out in the open. That would teach him to stalk me again. Begrudgingly I had to admit, if only to myself, that Tia was not wrong when she made me promise to park my rusty crotch rocket a couple of streets down from the mansion. That girl proved to be better at what I was than me. Not that it surprised me. The human was determined to tackle everything she came across with gusto until she was as good as she possibly could be at it.

Unlike me.

I got the theory of everything down to perfection due to reading and hunting information like a hound, but when it came to implementing it, I folded into the fetal position and tried to disappear. Not that I was a psychologist or anything, but I was pretty sure that was some sort of trauma rearing its ugly head. One I had every intention of ignoring for as long as I lived. Which wouldn't be long judging by the day and night I'd had so far.

After fifteen minutes or so, my feet started to shuffle around. My bladder didn't get the memo that someone might be lurking and waiting to kill me when Tia kept feeding me ice cubes under the excuse that it'd help me calm down. She was using some of it on her burned palm, and I was sure she only liked to watch me suffer and wince as I crunched on the cubes so I didn't have to argue with her. It also kept my mouth shut so she could talk.

The front door of the mansion opened silently, the light turning on and a bright yellow glow spilling over the front porch and steps like a river made of gold. I recognized the thin figure stepping over the threshold, although his features were covered in darkness from the light hitting his back. Master Bowmen looked too awake for this time of the night as he stopped at the top step and folded his hands at the small of his back. The casual way he was holding himself did not fool me when I could feel his magic reaching around us and prodding at my own.

He must've felt the presence, too.

Not surprisingly, after a few seconds the feeling of being watched disappeared like it was never there. Squaring my shoulders and stiffening my spine, I pushed away from the tree and strolled across the street with a confidence I didn't feel. My uncle watched every twitch of my muscles like a hawk, his burning gaze raising goosebumps over my skin.

"Target eliminated." Proud that I sounded the same as everyone I'd heard give reports after a mission, I didn't climb up to the porch. Instead, I craned my neck to meet his eyes.

Master Bowmen said nothing for a very long time, but I felt judged nonetheless. Keeping my knees locked and preventing myself from fidgeting was the hardest thing I'd ever done. One wrong blink of an eye and he would know I was lying. Hell, he might know I was lying now, regardless of all the practicing Tia made me do.

"Walk with me, nibbling." His deep voice carried an undercurrent of something I couldn't name when he descended the stairs and headed around the mansion.

It was a good thing he didn't shout liar straight away, right?

Shadows swallowed him when he rounded a corner, and I rushed behind to catch up with him. When I reached him, I fell into step, clutching my fists hard enough for my nails to rip the skin of my palms. *Deep breaths and don't talk too much. Only answer whatever you are asked with short, direct answers. Don't blabber.* Tia's voice echoed in my head and I bit my tongue because that was exactly what I wanted to do.

Blabber until I bored him to death and he told me to go away.

I really wanted to go away right now.

"You are so much like my sister." The softly spoken words when we reached the neatly trimmed rose shrubs, which were barely visible from the dim light coming from the side, made me stumble for a second before I caught myself. Master Bowmen chuckled at my clumsiness, shaking his head while I tried not to hyperventilate.

He didn't talk about my parents.

Offering only off-handed comments every time I used to pester him with questions, he would get angry and tell me to go away. Maybe the vampire did kill me and now I was in some sort of personal hell where my human friend had become some superhero sidekick and my uncle talked about my mother with affection in his voice.

That had to be it.

"She was like you at that age, too," Master Bowman continued, oblivious to my inner turmoil. "So eager to prove herself. Fast to rush to danger just to test her limits and get better than me in everything."

Too afraid that he would stop talking, I said nothing as I felt the heartbeat in my throat.

"She was a year"—Cocking his head to the side, he paused in thought—"maybe two younger than you when she eliminated her first target."

"She was?" The question was barely a breath passing my lips, but he heard me.

"Mhm, yes she was." Stopping in front of a shrub, he ripped a few leaves and shredded them between his fingers with nerve-wracking precision. "It changed her." His head turned to the side, and I could feel the weight of his gaze although his eyes were covered from the darkness. "When you have a kind heart, taking a life is never easy, no matter what you were born to be."

"I did what I had to do. It's what I am." Understanding that this was more of him testing my sanity than his willingness to share something personal made the idea of lying to him more bearable. "I always told you I'm the best assassin mage you have. You didn't believe me."

"Who was he?" When I didn't answer fast enough, Master Bowmen cleared his throat uncomfortably. "You are the only one to see his face and live. Who was he?"

Nigel's handsome face pushed to the forefront of my mind, muddling my brain. Then the scent of roses reached my nose, reminding me of the one he held in his hand and the thorn covered with my blood. I forced the bile down that was burning the roof of my mouth. With my heart beating like a war drum against my ribs, I took a deep breath and blew it out slowly.

"I've never seen him before in my life." That much was true.

Master Bowmen nodded once, as if he expected that answer but still had to ask. The silence that stretched between us had never been this uncomfortable. There was tension wafting off him that I could feel. It made my heartbeat speed up, which shouldn't be possible. My poor heart was already working on overdrive, and if it kept it up, I might faint right there in the bushes like some drunk.

"The news came an hour ago that Nigel Thatcher is dead." A bird chirped from a distance and I flinched from the sound. "I've never heard of a target being eliminated before one of my own told me the mission was done."

"You've never sent anyone after a ghost before either." Closing my mouth with an audible snap, I bit hard on my tongue. *Stupid. You are so stupid, Charlie. Keep your mouth shut you dumbnut.* The voice in my head sounded a lot like Tia, although she would've used a much better word than dumbnut, I was sure.

"You speak the truth." Master Bowmen pulled me out of my panicked thoughts. "I should've known if a situation called for untested tactics or an innovative approach to things you would be the best one for the job."

"What does that mean?" My narrowed eyes were wasted on him since he couldn't see me in the darkness.

"The usual, the routine ... it never worked for you." With a flick of his wrist he told me to get moving again as he turned around and headed to the front of the mansion, tucking his hands in the pockets of his pants. "You always need to be challenged in different ways. There is a need in you to prove that the impossible is very much possible. It's what makes you thrive."

"I'm finding it a little hard to see the compliment there." When he snorted, I got agitated. "It sounds like you are using nice words to call me difficult and complicated."

"Ordinary is boring, nibbling. Take it from someone that has tried to be it all his life. It's fear of being shunned that stops most of us from reaching our full potential." I finally saw his face when we rounded the corner, the yellow light illuminating his features. The softness in his gaze wobbled my knees. "You never had that fear, so don't start with it now."

"Only because I was shunned before I knew what all of that means." My chin jutted out stubbornly when he tried to shut me up with a look of pity. "I never cared and I won't start now."

"Good." Nodding, he touched my forearm to stop me from walking. "Keep that in mind because you will need it."

"Need it for what?" When he kept watching me with no

answer, dread pooled like lead in my stomach. "I will need it for what?"

"I must ward off your magic again tonight. The old wards won't do."

"What? No!" Taking a step back, the heel of my boot hit the edge on the uneven steppingstone and my arms wind-milled to keep me from ending up on my back. "Stay away from me."

Master Bowmen grabbed my shirt, yanking me straight with a determined look. His lips turned into a thin white line that blended in with all the wrinkles on his face. Fear that he would block my magic at a time I was in debt to a vampire and had to break into the mage's guild made me irrational, and I barely stopped myself from attacking him by flinging my swords at him.

"Keep quiet." Hissing at me, he looked around to make sure no one was eavesdropping. "You need this if you want to stay alive, you stupid girl."

"I am alive." Hissing right back, I jerked away from his grip.

"You won't be alive tonight if he senses that you have magic."

"If who senses that I have magic?" But I knew. Before my uncle even opened his mouth to form the words I knew who *he* was. Dark spots danced at the corners of my vision, and Master Bowmen's face looked like it was too far away.

"To honor our success, The Magician is having a ball at the mage's guild tonight. The invitation arrived along with the note of thank you for eliminating the target." Eyes darting around, he stepped close enough I could smell the scent of the soap he used on his skin. "Or, I don't have to ward anything if you simply disappear. Those sent to look for you will be strongly advised not to find you."

The Magician

I didn't think I was ready for yet another bomb to drop on my head this day.

Color me surprised, but I was still standing, although the ground opened under my feet in hopes to swallow me whole. He wanted me to run. My own flesh and blood was chasing me away from the only home I'd known. Not because of fear as he would like me to believe. I could see it in the depths of his irises while he stared at me eagerly as if expecting to be obeyed without question. He really never spent time getting to know me, not even a little. I might be clumsy and a horrible assassin mage, but I smelled bull crap from miles away. Nothing could hide the resentment shining through his eyes, or the greed of a person that wanted something so bad it hurt, though that same person could never have it. My magic always had that effect on Master Bowmen. I'd seen it enough times to recognize it instantly.

Something was fishy with all this. Everything was too well aligned, and although I knew Nigel wouldn't leave anything to chance to reach his goal, I didn't think the vampire was an almighty force that could bring all the parties into perfect sync. The story the vampire told me about the Necronomicon didn't sound like a myth anymore. Nothing short of that would get powerful males like my uncle, Nigel, and the Magician all playing a game of cat and mouse like this.

Tia was right. I might need a sidekick after all, because what I was about to do was a suicide mission. If that damn thing existed, I was going to make sure none of the greedy sons of a nutcracker got their hands on it. I would steal the Necronomicon and make sure no one ever found it again.

I'd destroy the book.

"Ward off my magic." It was comical to see the shock

on Master Bowman's face. "Hurry up, I have a ball I have to attend and I need some sleep before it."

Chapter Thirteen

"I would have eyes in the back of my head if I were you tonight," Jonas, the dimwit, muttered from beside me in the back of the long-stretch limousine.

"Remind me again, why are you here?" Subtly wiping my sweat-covered palms off the leather seat so I didn't stain the silk of my dress, I glared at Jonas. "If I'm not mistaken, it says on the door no pets allowed." The hatred burning in his gaze made me smile.

The mage's guild came into view and I craned my neck as I huddled near the window to get a better look. We were moving slowly, a long line of black limousines inching closer to the entrance as soon as the occupants of the leading one exited and swaggered to the wide-open front doors. Hollywood had nothing on the arrogance of mages. Everything had to be flashy and in your face. I made the mistake of pointing out to Master Bowmen that The Magician must be compensating for something. Up to this day he wouldn't let me talk in front of people if he could help it, and it was all because of that comment.

"Now is not the time to bicker among ourselves," my uncle reprimanded from his seat across from us, though he wouldn't meet my eyes. Poor Glenda fidgeted next to him, looking like she was ready to bolt. "Let us not give anyone a reason to believe we have discord, or to start paying closer attention to our clan. Nothing good ever comes from that."

In other words, we all needed to smile and nod even when we were being insulted.

"I still don't understand why I had to dress up in this." Plucking at the long skirt of the silk dress, I pursed my lips in annoyance. "I should be with the rest of them waiting for you to arrive. Am I not the reason we are here?"

All assassin mage's from my clan that have successfully completed missions were already inside the guild. Dressed in our usual attire of all black, only this time with the emblem of my clan—two dragons twisting around each other—etched on their backs, they were lined up like soldiers waiting on Master Bowmen. Truth or not, thanks to Nigel, I should be there too, face and hair covered and resembling a statue. Not waiting here exposed, dressed up like a spoiled brat in silks with crystals dangling from my ears like ornaments. The only consolation I had was that Jonas the dumbnut was here too, dressed in a tux and looking like he had a stick stuck in his butt.

I deserved to be covered, damn it.

My lie worked.

"Do not question me," Master Bowmen hissed at me before flattening invisible wrinkles on his immaculate suit. "All you have to do tonight is nod, smile, and say thank you. Am I clear?"

"Like a swamp," I deadpan, flinching as soon as the words were out. Under his unwavering glare, I ground my teeth and cleared my throat. "Understood."

"I will make sure she follows orders." Jonas was fast to jump on the opportunity to get on my nerves. "It's my honor to serve the needs of my clan."

Master Bowmen was already nodding his agreement when Glenda shocked the hell out of all of us by speaking up. "I will stay with Charlie and make sure everything goes smoothly."

We all turned to her like she just grew a second head, and she wiggled on the seat nervously but stood her ground. Delicately clearing her throat and giving us a shrug, she didn't look away from my uncle.

"Jonas makes her angry, while I keep her calm." With each word her voice grew more confident, and I couldn't help but smile at her. "We all know angry Charlie means a lot of trouble. Or lots of fire we need to put out."

"Hey!" The smile slipped and I scowled at her. "No need to be rude. I don't do it on purpose."

"No kibitzer, you are just that incapable of living up to what nature made you to be." Jonas slipped with his name calling, earning himself a look of disgust from my uncle. The dimwit blanched, opening his mouth no doubt to apologize, but Master Bowmen cut him off with a sharp look.

"Jonas will go with me. Glenda, you stay with Charlie, and if anything goes wrong tonight, I will hold you both accountable."

The door of the limousine opened just as my uncle finished talking. Bright lights coming from the entrance of the guild blinded me, illuminating the dark interior I was accustomed to seeing. Blinking like an owl, I did my best to swallow my heart down, the damn thing fluttering like a bird that was fighting to escape a cage in my chest.

Jonas was the first to move, gracefully twisting his tall frame like a snake and exiting the vehicle. He stepped to the side with his back to us as he waited for my uncle to join him. After shooting me a pointed look, Master Bowmen was next, with Glenda crawling across the long leather seat in her rush to follow. I didn't think I could unglue my butt from my own seat to move, little less get out of the car.

"Charlie?" I blinked Glenda's face into clarity when she ducked her head inside, a small smile playing on her lips. "Everything will be okay," she whispered, offering me her hand.

Staying locked in her gaze, I took her offered palm and let her tug me out of the limousine. The silk of the dress felt too hot on my chilled, pebbled skin when the cold breeze of Elizabet River washed over me. Shivering, I did my best not to hug my body and hunched my shoulders. The pale blue silk complimented my skin tone, but the thin straps and low, open back did nothing to cover my markings. Black lines swirled on every exposed inch, something I should proudly fling in everyone's face like a peacock fanning its tail. I'd done everything I could to hide them, so being displayed like this makes me feel strange.

Vulnerable.

If my uncle noticed my discomfort, he didn't show it. Plastering a pleasant smile on his withered face, he stepped toward the open doors with an even, unhurried pace. Jonas fell into step behind him and slightly off to his left. On wobbly knees, my poor ankles screaming in the strappy sandals, I let Glenda guide me on their heels. My fingers started twitching and I felt the sting of magic under my skin ready to burst at any moment if I felt threatened or something spooked me out. I shouldn't have messed with the wards Master Bowmen placed. I regret removing them now.

Not a good thing.

Focusing on my breathing, I pushed everything away.

Every thought, every doubt ... All I had to do was go through the night for a few hours and get the hell out of here. I'd figure out a way to sneak in and snatch the book while every mage in the building was otherwise occupied, then I'd get the hell out of dodge. Nigel would love to hear that, I bet. Speaking of which.

My gaze darted around as inconspicuously as I possibly could make it while I searched for the bloodsucker, but I could neither see or feel him anywhere. I'd bet my magic that he was nearby and keeping an eye on his investment. Butterflies erupted in a frenzy in my belly at the thought, and I angrily stomped on them. *Down girl, he is just as bad as the rest of them,* I told my body, but it didn't listen to me when it came to the vampire. It had a mind of its own.

The mage's guild opened up before me as I walk through the doors. Tall ceilings loomed over shiny floors covered in tiles clean enough to do your makeup on. The crystal chandeliers swayed gently, by a spell no doubt, reflecting a rainbow of colors over everyone present. The hundreds of small lightbulbs could be seen on the ground, and it felt like I was walking on stars as I strode into the large space. Tables were sprinkled in the room, each one set for ten people each, while chairs draped with silver fabric were positioned around them. Creatures from all fictions were gathered in groups, laughing and talking about everything and nothing at the same time. The voices were like the buzzing of a cloud of bees to my ears. Magic saturated the air, choking me.

I didn't belong here.

Panic gripped me and I started turning to dart out of the damn place. My uncle was right. I should run, not come willingly to this snake pit. Small, cold fingers latched onto my forearm, the nails digging into my skin. My head snapped to the side to see Glenda's pale face as she frantically shook her head, not hard enough to be seen but visible enough to look like she was about to have a seizure. She snatched a glass off the tray one of the waiters carried like a trophy in front of his face and pressed it into my palm.

"We need to talk," she spat the words under her breath. "Now."

"Everything alright there?" My uncle turned to look at both of us over his shoulder, his eyebrows scrunched over his eyes like caterpillars.

"Restroom," Glenda blurted before she shrunk back, her face turning bright red.

Not wanting to get her in trouble, I yanked my forearm out of her clutches and linked my arm through hers. "We must use to restroom so we don't miss anything important." Trying for nonchalance, I waved the flute Glenda gave me, sloshing the drink all over my hand. My uncle's lips blended in with his wrinkles. "We'll be right back, nervous bladders."

Ignoring Jonas and his hateful glare, I dragged poor Glenda along with me in a random direction. Master Bowmen cleared his throat, and when I glanced at him, he pointedly looked to the opposite side. The one that had a huge sign saying restrooms with an arrow pointing at a hallway. With a tight smile, I switched direction as if that was where I was going in the first place. Good thing I was holding onto Glenda when my ankle twisted and stars burst in front of my eyes. Leaning heavily on her arm, I wobbled us into the hallway and out of sight.

"Mother fudge!" Whisper-yelling in the empty hallway, I released Glenda and yanked the long skirt of the dress up to my knees. "That is going to swell up, you watch." Lifting my poor ankle, I prodded at it gingerly with my forefinger.

"I know what you are planning to do." My tearful gaze snapped to Glenda's face, all pain forgotten. "I saw it in one of my visions."

"Shut up." Hissing at her, I looked around, praying that no one heard her. "What's wrong with you?"

Her eyes bugged out when I grabbed her by the upper arm and wrestled her inside the restroom. After making sure no one else was there, banging doors of stalls and checking every nook and cranny, I turned to face her with a glare. The green dress she was wearing made her skin whiter than snow and her hair redder than flames. If I didn't know she was a seer, I would've guessed she was one of the fae. Her delicate features, just like Tia's, didn't really fit with the rest of us.

"You are talking nonsense that can get us both killed." Folding my arms across my chest, I stared her down.

"Am I?" All signs of the fragile seer were gone as she lifted her chin stubbornly. "I know what I saw, and that's the only reason I begged Master Bowmen to let me come tonight."

"You wanted to be here?" My jaw dropped before I reminded myself that was the last of my worries. "I plan on doing nothing apart from staying out of The Magician's way."

"Right, we can pretend that you are not about to attempt the greatest theft in history of the world."

My mouth opened then closed several times before I sighed, my shoulders dropping in defeat. I could argue with her until tomorrow, but there was knowledge in the depths of her eyes that couldn't be faked. It was one of the reasons she got picked on in the clan. She called everyone out in their lies because she already knew the many outcomes to every situation. Instead of being stupid like the rest of them, maybe I could use this to my advantage.

"I was actually thinking of leaving ... for good," I confessed.

"I know, but that is the wrong path for you, Charlie." Encouraged by my acceptance of her gift, she moved eagerly closer. "I shouldn't get involved because it will change things, and then where would we be? But I can nudge, you know. You are a bright bulb, so you'll get my hints."

"Thanks, Glenda. I've always dreamed to be called a bright bulb." She giggled like a little girl at my snark.

"If you run you will die." The blood curdled in my veins, ice shards stabbing my heart. "You need to see this through. It's the only way forward."

"And if I do go forward?" A million things rushed to the front of my mind, things I'd like to ask yet didn't want to hear the answer to.

"All will be as it should be if you stay on the course you've chosen." Her teeth worry her bottom lip so hard I thought she'd bite through it.

"What is it that you are not telling me?" Glancing at the clock above the mirrors, I realized we'd been there too long. My uncle would get suspicious.

"I can't ..." Her head shook in frustration and there was desperation in her eyes. "I'm not supposed to say anything, but ..."

"But what? We need to get back. Come on, give me something. Anything." It looked like I was as desperate as she wass and I didn't know it.

"Whatever you do Charlie ..." Swallowing thickly, Glenda looked like she'd be sick. I glided a little further away just in case. "No matter the situation, or whatever the case may be, don't open the book. Promise me."

"I promise." My voice cracked from the hard beating of my heart. That was an easy promise to make. I had no intention on doing anything other than destroying it.

When nothing else was said, I guided Glenda out of the restroom with a hand pressed between her shoulder blades. The poor thing could barely see where she was going. It took a moment to realize that there was a reason she looked dazed when she gasped and blinked her eyes clear. Locking them on my face, she gave me a smile that raised goosebumps on my arms.

"The one you think is an enemy will be the one to save you from yourself."

"What?" My mind going straight to The Magician, I frowned at her. Like hell that son of a biscuit eater would save me from anything.

"The blade is only as sharp as the hand that wields it." Petting my arm, she walked away with a small giggle. "You will be fine Charlie Jansen, just don't open the book."

Chapter Fourteen

I could feel their creepy-crawler eyes following the markings on my skin as I weaved through the crowd looking for Master Bowmen. Glenda's head bobbed a few feet in front of me, making it easy to avoid the curious people around me. My uncle might be the smartest person I knew by exposing me like this, or he wanted me dead since he claimed I had no magic. Or barely any, in any case.

The living wall of black-clad assassin mages parted when we reached my clan, revealing my uncle and Jonas conversing animatedly with someone. The man had his back to me, his broad shoulders stretching the fabric of his tux just right so it molded to the rest of his body. The prickling at the back of my neck should've been enough warning, but I was too busy checking the guy's butt out to notice. I jerked to a stop when a body blocked my view, my nose almost bumping into the starched-white shirt of the person's chest.

"Charlie Jansen." The man cutting my path drawled,

the sweetness in his voice sickening in its falseness. My eyes dragged up his shoulders and neck to lock on pale green ones full of disdain. "We finally meet."

All the blood drained from my body, leaving me numb and frozen in place.

"You do look very much like your mother, if I remember her correctly." The Magician smiled, a malicious curl of his thin lips daring me to call him out on his wrongs.

He looked much younger than his age. Actually, he looked exactly the same as he did all those years ago when he killed my parents. Not a line could be found on the smooth skin of his face, like no time had passed. A hooked nose sat between his pale green eyes, the neatly trimmed eyebrows slashing straight above them. His thin frame was hidden by the expensive tux he had on, the blood-red handkerchief in his breast pocket the only stark color on his washed-up appearance. Only slightly taller than me, he was at the perfect height for me to crack his acorns if I lifted my knee.

I really wanted to lift my knee.

Anger bathed everything in a red haze.

"There you are, Charlie." My uncle materialized by my side, his knobby hands latching onto my arm in a painful grip. "I was just about to ask Jonas to come find you. I have someone I'd like you to meet." Pretending that he just noticed the monster in front of me, Master Bowmen sucked in a breath. "Oh dear, I apologize. I did not see who my niece was talking to."

"It is not a bother." The Magician sniffed, eating up my uncle's groveling like it was his God given right. "I thought it appropriate to introduce myself personally, given that she is the star of the night and all."

My mouth opened, but it snapped shut so I could grind my teeth when my uncle tightened his hold so hard I could feel the skin on my arm ripping under his nails. I got the message. Keep my mouth shut. Not that I was planning to listen to it.

"So humble of you, Sir." Master Bowmen inclined his head, and if he lowered it just a little more he could kiss the monster's navel. "She is very young and unaware of the importance of decorum, I'm afraid."

"Don't mention it." Flicking his wrist, The Magician drilled my skull with his intent gaze. "We were all young and stupid once, as the humans like to say." His, as well as my uncle's laughter sounded forced.

I didn't laugh.

"Indeed." Master Bowman chuckled nervously, his eyes going over The Magician's shoulder. A real smile stretched his lips. "I think you would be happy to see the person I wanted to introduce to my niece as well, Sir." A shadow fell over us as the said person moved to join us, and I was grateful for my uncle's punishing hold on me when my knees weakened and I wobbled on my heels. "You know Blade if I'm not mistaken."

Nigel, mother trucking, Thatcher stepped up next to me pretending he had never seen me in his life. The Magician caught me off guard because it was the vampire's butt I was staring at so hard that I wasn't paying attention. It felt like someone just sucked all the oxygen from the room. I couldn't breathe.

"Long time, old friend." I watched stunned, my jaw hitting the floor when the vampire and The Magician clasped forearms and slapped each other on the back.

"Too long if you ask me." The monster snickered as he

leaned closer to Nigel. "But worth it since we got rid of our problem I'd say, hey?"

"Very true," Nigel chirped. I was confused as hell.

What was happening here?

"Blade, I'd like to introduce my niece, Charlie Jansen of the Jansen clan." Master Bowmen tugged me forward, and I dangled from his hand like he was presenting a slave to be sold. "Charlie, this is a good friend to the mage's guild. We would not have been successful if he didn't help with insights about your target."

Owlishly blinking at Nigel, I watched him in slow motion as he took my numb fingers and brought them to his lips. "Charmed," he murmured, his lips grazing the skin of my knuckles. "She is a sight to behold."

"Just like her mother." The Magician sneered, and something inside me broke.

"Excuse us." My voice was like a whip snapping between the three of them.

Yanking out of my uncle's hold, I snatched Nigel's arm and manhandled him through the crowd. He allowed it, chuckling and waving my uncle off when he gasped and tried to stop me. I was beyond caring if everyone found out that the son of a cracked nut was alive. Fury burned my insides like lava, and my magic burst through my fingertips in short sparks. When I reached the tall glass floor-to-ceiling windows overlooking the river, I jerked him to a stop and planted both fists on my hips. I was so angry no words formed on my tongue. I could only gape at him like a fish pulled out of the water.

"What can I do for you, Ms. Jansen?" His British accent thickened and those gray eyes bored into mine before very slowly rolling up and down my body with so much intensity I could feel it like a physical touch.

"What are you doing here?" The question was like spitting venom at the dumbnut. Not that it made a difference.

He chuckled, the deep masculine sound pebbling my skin.

"Why, enjoying our victory, of course." The slight stiffening of his shoulders was the only sign I needed to know we were not alone anymore.

"A problem, Blade?" Jonas joined us, his beady eyes narrowed on my face.

"Not until you showed up," I chirped, giving him a too-sweet smile. "What do you want Jonas? You are stretching your leash too tight."

People were trying to be subtle while keeping the drama we were causing in view, even if they had to see it from the corner of their eyes. Whispers spread like a wave around us, and I knew I shouldn't take the bait when it came to Jonas, but I couldn't help myself. I was stretched thin already, and I couldn't handle much more past what I'd dealt with the past two days. The idiot had enough too, because his hand closed around my upper arm, my magic perking at the contact. Before I could blast him to smithereens and betray my uncle's lie of me not having magic, Nigel growled deep in his throat, the sound freezing Jonas in his tracks.

"Release her." The words were so softly spoken they triggered my fight or flight instincts. "This instant."

"I meant no offense, Blade." Backtracking fast, Jonas paled and dropped my arm like it burned him. "Master Bowmen wanted to make sure everything was well."

"We are perfectly fine. Isn't that the truth, Ms. Jansen?"

"Yeah." Glowering at Jonas, I took a deep breath. "Perfectly fine."

With one last suspicious glance my way, Jonas walked away, leaving me with the vampire. The interruption lasted long enough to allow me to calm a little, but a bit of agitation still simmered in my chest. I felt like a rabbit released in the woods so the wolves could chase it and play with it until it got tired, only to kill it without remorse when they got bored. There I went again with the silly rabbits. I should call the hotel to tell them to remove those glass statues. Pushing the thought aside, I turned to face Nigel, who was watching me with too much interest for my liking.

"If you had access to the guild, why aren't you taking it yourself?" No need to spell out what *it* was since we both already knew.

"If I could, you don't think I would have by now?" One eyebrow cocked, which only added to the allure of his intriguing features he prodded. "Say it. What is it that you want, Ms. Jansen?"

That was a good question, wasn't it? What was it that I wanted? Telling him what I was going to do and how it'd mess up all of their plans would be very satisfying, if only to see the look on his face. Since I couldn't do that and walk out of there alive, I opted for the second best thing. Distraction.

"I need to disappear for a while without making my uncle suspicious." It was fascinating watching his lips twitch at the corners. "You think you can help with that?"

"I believe I might have some brilliant ideas, yes." Nigel lifted his hand to my face, tucking a loose strand behind my ear.

His gray irises darkened, and he trailed his knuckles lightly over my cheek and down my neck, stopping too long for comfort at the spot he drew blood with the rose before continuing to my collar bone. Goosebumps followed the path of his touch, and I hated that my body reacted to it the way it did when what I really wanted was to punch him in the face. Leaning close enough that I could feel his breath fanning the side of my face, I felt a morbid thrill when his breath hitched from my nearness.

Two could play this game.

Well two could've played it if my elbow didn't give out where I was leaning on his forearm, and I tilted to the side as gravity pulled me to the floor. My heart jumped up and it hit the roof of my mouth when vertigo attacked, a squeak lodging in my throat that was unable to come out. A strong arm wrapped around my waist and I found myself pressed tightly to a firm, muscular chest, the scent of sin and darkness filling my nostrils from Nigel's skin.

"Careful there, love." His deep voice rumbled in my ear. "I'll start thinking I'm making your knees weak."

Leave it to Nigel Thatcher to be so full of himself.

The man had never heard the word humble in his long life.

Pushing on his chest to get away from him was as futile as a fly trying to move an elephant. The last time I tried to get physical like this with the vampire, I didn't remember him being this strong. Did my blood do this or was he holding back in the hotel? Nothing made sense when it came to Nigel, and that was one thing that drove me insane. Everything made sense if you knew enough about it. The problem was, no one had useful information about a ghost. One that apparently hung around being everyone's best buddy while they were celebrating his death.

Go figure.

"I believe this will be the perfect timing for it Ms. Jansen." he said, snaring me in his gaze when I looked up at him.

"Huh?" I wasn't sure I said it loud enough because I was too busy getting lost in the gray of his eyes.

"I am happy to oblige," Nigel murmured in a rough voice, then his mouth crushed to mine.

Everything around me disappeared. People, danger, my uncle, as well as the man I hated the most in the world, The Magician. All of it was a distant memory that faded away when Nigel grazed the seam of my lips with the tip of his tongue, searching for entrance. My mouth parted to allow him to sweep in, and his taste exploded in my mouth. A soft, pathetic moan ripped from my chest, and his answering groan was punctuated by the tightening of his arm around my waist. I lost track of place and time, and when he started pulling away, I chased his lips, not daring to open my eyes. He chuckled softly, giving me a soft peck on my kiss-swollen lips. With great effort, my eyelids opened and my breath was taken away from the look in his eyes. The smirk playing on his glistening mouth would've made me angry if I could actually think straight.

"I suggest you use this opportunity to go to the powder room so you can collect yourself, Ms. Jansen," he whispered in my ear, and it was like he poured a bucket of cold water over my head.

I jerked away from his arms.

"Charlie?" The scandalized way my uncle said my name from behind me made me want to die of embarrassment. "Charlie Jansen," he snapped just before he reached us.

"Distraction." Nigel shrugs nonchalantly, his smirk growing.

"Excuse me, I'll be right back." Ducking my head because my face was burning, I darted around my uncle as fast as my feet would carry me, accidently bumping into a waiter and sending him and his tray full of hors d'oeuvres flying through the air to shower over the people gawking at Nigel's display.

I swore I heard Nigel telling my uncle that I was young and easily impressed.

I'd show him easily impressed when I dump the ashes of the book at his feet.

We would see who would be impressed then.

Chapter Fifteen

Pressing my wet hands to my cheeks to cool them, I stared at my face in the mirror. Hiding in the restrooms was not going to help, but I was too shaken to move. The hand on the clock above me kept creeping up, and it only reminded me that as bad as Nigel's distraction was, I still didn't have too much time to lose. I had no idea where to start searching to begin with.

The door to the restroom opened and a couple of ladies walked in, shifters by the build of their bodies and the inner glow of their eyes. Their envious and pitying glances were enough to get me out of that place. I wasn't sure if I got them because Nigel kissed me, or because they knew who my uncle was. It could be either at that point. With a mumbled "Sorry," I brushed past them and closed the door behind me, leaning back on it.

Voices drifted from down the hallway, but thankfully no one lingered here.

The clinking of glasses reached my ears just as one of the waiters came from around the corner, the large tray in his hands wobbling in his palms. Excited to see him coming from the opposite side of where everyone was gathered, I gave him a huge smile. Flinching, his eyes dropped to my visible makings and he rushed past me, spilling drinks all over the tray and himself. With a sigh, my head dipped low on my shoulders. It was a wonderful feeling to be judged by something you had no control over. Not.

Pushing off the door, I squared my shoulders and walked down the hallway like I knew where I was going. *Fake it till you make it and all that*, I thought with a smirk. If anyone saw me and asked, I'd just act like I got lost. If they had seen the vampire taking advantage of the situation earlier, no one would doubt me because they'd think I wasn't smart enough to know my way around. With that in mind, I moved around the guild, the twisting hallways and winding stairways leading me nowhere important. Everywhere I turned, locked doors or storage areas with an occasional empty office met me. There was no trace of strong magic either. Whatever lingered in the air was just a remnant from all the mages spending hours upon hours in this place. Just as I was about to give up, the faint sound of buzzing came from behind me.

Whirling around, I searched for whatever had made the sound, but there was nothing there. Moving slowly, I strained my ears and tried to pinpoint its location, until I found myself facing a wall. The sound of turning gears continued and grew louder where I stood, so I pressed my hand to the wall before doing the same with my ear. The sound echoed like the building was hollow behind the wall. Rapping my knuckles on it gently told me I was right. It sounded like an elevator moving, but I didn't remember seeing one. Everywhere I searched I only found stairs.

Keeping my palm on the wall, I moved down the hallway, pausing occasionally to see if I was getting closer or further from it by the strength of the vibrations My palm caressed the wall. I knew I found it before I saw the door because of the strong urge to rip it open almost doubling me over. I'd never felt anything like it before, so I panted through clenched teeth until I had enough strength to straighten. The cold sweat made the silk of the dress cling to my skin, but I ignored it and ran my hands around the door to search for a button. There had to be a way to call the elevator, but I could find nothing apart from a smooth wall. Huffing in annoyance, I took a step back while eyeing the door.

The annoyed huff coming from around a corner was my saving grace. Panicked, I darted into the first room I could get in and held the door open just a crack so I could see who made the noise. My ears were buzzing from the drumming of my heart. That was a very close call. A mage, judging by the ball of light hovering above his palm, walked into view, stopping in front of the elevator door. I couldn't be that lucky, could I? To my delight, he made the light dissipate by drawing a sigil with his hand across the door. The symbol lit up like fireworks, so I burned it into my memory.

The door whooshed open to allow him entrance, and a moment later he was gone. I stood still, deciding to wait a bit longer in case he had a friend coming, but when no one else showed up, I shoved the door open and stepped out. With a smile on my face, I rushed to my way up, and when I heard no gears, I drew the sigil as well. I had only a few seconds to admire my work and feel proud of myself because the next second, magic exploded out of it, hitting me in the center of the chest and slamming me on the opposite wall. My skull cracked from the impact and stars burst behind my eyes.

Magic drenched the air, suffocating me.

Pounding footsteps got me moving as fast as I could. With a groan, I pushed myself off the floor and stumbled inside the now open door into the elevator. With my heart in my throat, I screamed inside my head. *Come on, come on. I made it this far. I can't get caught now.* The door closed and my stomach plunged when I shot in the air faster than I expected. Knees bent, I waited until I reached my destination—whatever it may be. I brought my magic under my skin in case I needed to fight my way out when the door opened. The running I heard downstairs was definitely not an exercise at a PT class. They knew someone was breaking in. How much time did that give me? The sound of breaking wood and plaster from below announced I didn't have much. Probably five, ten minutes tops if they had to climb up here while dangling from the metal ropes moving the elevator up and down.

"You got this Charlie." My pep talk didn't help at all. No, it just made my hands shake like I'd developed arthritis all of a sudden. "Fiddlesticks. I really had to get myself in this mess, didn't I?"

Jerking to a stop, I almost ended up sprawled on the metal floor, my poor shoulder and elbow stopping that disaster but smarting like a son of a gun when they slammed into the side wall and handrail. The door slid open with a soft ding, and my swords snapped out in my hands. A gaping pitch-black hole greeted me from the other side, the silence coming from it deafening in its intensity. Or it could be because I was freaked out of my wits and I was seeing monsters crawling all over the place. With trembling hands and holding my breath, I inched closer, but the door closed too fast and I was sent stumbling back when the elevator shot up again.

Just how tall was this building?

Looking from the outside it was just like any business tower, lost in a sea of metal and glass in the city. Not too tall to draw attention but tall enough to make sure everyone knew not to mess with it. Standing trapped in the metal box taking me who knew where, it felt like I was inside the tallest building in the world. Cold sweat trickled down my spine and soaked into my dress. I was going to look like a wreck survivor if I managed to get out of here alive. *When*, I corrected in my head. *When I get out of here alive.*

Be it as it may, I had no intention on dying tonight.

Not if I could help it.

For the second time, the elevator jerked to a stop and I braced myself for an attack as soon as the door started sliding open. The darkness from my first stop called to something deep inside me, luring me to search for it like a siren song. I had no delusions that I mistook the feeling for what it was. Ancient, powerful magic was present there, and I knew it was where I needed to be. After I dealt with whoever brought me here.

A red and golden glow reached my eyes and dimly illuminated the space. Four mages stood like a living shield to block my exit, their hands alight with offensive magic. The fires crackled and spat from their palms, casting shadows over their stern faces and making them look more menacing than they had a right to be. A nervous snort exploded from my lips, triggering a chain reaction.

I guessed we were all a little too tense at the moment.

Trigger happy, if you would.

Cornered inside the metal confines of the elevator, I didn't have much space to work with, and although my magic had always acted weird when I'd tried to use it, I could always count on it to go a little nuts when I was spooked and destroy everything around me. Take that, Master Bowmen.

Two large balls of fire sailed for my head and I ducked to avoid them, flinging one of my swords blindly at the mass of bodies crowding the open door. The smell of roasted meat filled the space around me, and to my shame, my stomach grumbled like an angry beast. I might've puked a little knowing it was the burning flesh of one of the mages that ended up skewered on my sword. The shriek of pain was swallowed by the rushing of blood in my ears. Pressing my back just to the side of the open entrance, I kept flinging magic as it came, hoping to keep them from entering the elevator. If all of us were stuffed inside like sardines, I'd kill myself right along with them. My magic was kind like that, and it didn't discriminate.

Another blast of magic came from the side, that one grazing my arm and my side and burning a hole in the dress. It just added to the wreck survivor image. My thought almost made me chuckle, but the pain was so much I had to grit my teeth to stop from screaming out. The markings wrapped around my torso flare up and healed my skin instantly, though it didn't take the pain away. No, it was festering under the freshly healed skin and beating with its own heartbeat. Calling the sword I threw at the mages, I sighed when its familiar weight settled in my palm. Hiding huddled in the corner would do me no good, so I clenched my jaw and called on all the magic I possibly could.

With a feral shout I rushed the door.

My ankle twisted, the heel of my sandal lodging itself in the space between the elevator and the floor I was on. My feral shout turned into an embarrassing squeak and my heart jumped, sticking itself to the roof of my mouth. *This is how I will die,* I think in my panic as I tripped over my own feet. Arms shooting to the sides to keep my balance, I pitched forward and barreled through four bodies that were trying to shoulder their way in. My boob popped out of my dress when the strap slid down my shoulder, the chilled air puckering my nipple. In the hysteria, I started praying that I wouldn't end up surviving this because I didn't want to be called the one-boob assassin mage.

Magic exploded from the center of my chest, bowing my back.

The weight of the bodies pressing all around me was flung away, which sent me faceplanting on the cold floor. With a loud grunt, all the air was pushed out of my lungs, my poor boobs hitting the ground so hard they almost end up popping out of my back. Especially the bare one. Static buzzed around my body, my hair lifting up in the air resembling Medusa's snakes when the strands started twisting and spitting residual magic.

"Owweee." I sounded pathetic to my own ears, the word coming out in a whisper.

The only answer was crackling of fires in the open space.

Shoving off the floor on trembling arms, I pushed my hair out of my face, looking around dazed. With numb fingers, I tugged the strap of the dress over my shoulder to cover my exposed flesh, the silk scraping over my skin like sandpaper.

I felt raw.

Undone.

Cages lined a massive open floor, thankfully all of them empty apart from one in the corner that unfortunately had some small animal inside. Its body was charred, small flames still dying all over it. Just like the four large lumps in twisted heaps that used to be mages.

Alive mages.

Acid burned the back of my throat. For a person who had no intention of killing anyone, my body count sure kept growing. The door chimed faintly, announcing it was about to close, so I crawled on all fours backward to stop it, not taking my eyes off the dead bodies. *What have I done?* The fact that they would've killed me if they had the chance was not important. I did break in here, after all, so they'd had every right to defend their territory. Me, on the other hand ...

I was just a killer.

And my time was up.

I needed to find that book and destroy it before I died. Because after this, there was no doubt in my mind that I was not getting out of here alive. If the Magician and his lackeys didn't kill me, the guilt eating my insides would do the job.

I needed to get to the lower level before that happened.

Chapter Sixteen

Getting back inside the elevator, I leaned heavily on one wall, the icy surface burning my skin. Numb all over, my unseeing eyes stared unblinkingly at the door that closed. All sound disappeared leaving me with the stench of burning bodies filling my nostrils.

Nothing happened.

The elevator didn't move, and no one could be heard banging on the door to get to me ...

Nothing.

I wished someone would pound on it to tell me they were alive.

Jerking in fear when the gears grind and squeal as I started descending, I absentmindedly smoothed my wild hair as if my appearance was the most important thing at the moment. I probably resembled a feral creature that hadn't seen civilization for years after that mess upstairs.

"At least you still have two boobs." My voice echoed in the tight confines and my giggle sounded strained and crazed.

Too soon I came to a stop, the ancient magic I felt earlier already caressing my senses. If it was any other time, I would've been more alert and wary from it. As things were, all I wanted to do was find where it was coming from and destroy the cursed thing. Destroy it before someone destroyed me. Sounded great in theory, but life had taught me that wasn't always the case in practice. There were always loops and turns that you had to go through.

Nothing was ever easy.

At least for me.

No sooner than I finished the thought the door opened, the darkness from the other side patiently waiting to eat me alive. It was how I saw it anyway. Being born as what I was, shadows had always been my friend. Inviting and feeling like home.

Safe.

It was in the darkness that safety could be found. It was also where I was most alone. Even shadows left in the darkness. Realizing that I was only making things more difficult by overthinking everything, I inched closer to the exit. A phantom breeze ruffled the tangled strands of my hair until they caressed my face. I was either going insane or I swore I could hear it whisper in a language I'd never heard before. Goosebumps popped out all over my arms and a shiver crawled up and down my spine. Swallowing thickly, I stepped out of the elevator.

The door closed with a resounding snap at my back.

I jumped a foot off the ground, twisting around to be met with smooth walls and no escape in sight. Short puffs of air came out of my lips, and I had to press both hands to my chest in hopes to slow my heart, which was doing its best to punch a hole through my chest. Gasping for breath like I was would have me fainting in no time. Being unable to see anything didn't help either, so I focused on one thing at a time. Slow my breathing so I could use my magic to bring some light in here.

"You got this, Charlie," I murmured under my breath.

Deep breath in. Hold it. Slow breath out.

In all that time, I couldn't stop thinking that Nigel met his end the same way as I was about to. It was his damn fault I was in this mess to begin with. If by some miracle I did survive, I was planning on becoming the biggest pain in his butt. He wouldn't be able to tinkle without me breathing down his neck. See how he liked that.

Dim light came from behind me, growing in intensity the longer I blinked like a fool to adjust to the brightness. With terror pooling in the pit of my stomach, I spun very slowly on my heels, dreading seeing what had created it. If more mages were gathered there waiting on me, I wasn't sure I could find it in me to fight them. To add more bodies to my list. To my great relief, not a soul could be found. The space seemed narrower and much smaller from the higher floor with the cages. The glow lighting my way was coming from sigils painted around the walls, every empty space used to its full capacity. There were hundreds of them.

Thousands even.

In my turn to face the room, I moved slightly forward and almost screamed when magic ropes manifested, coming alive before my eyes. They stretched from one wall to the other, connecting and entwining around each other like a cobweb. Gaps wide enough to barely squeeze through were taunting me when a bright golden sigil burst to life, illuminating an inconspicuous book propped on a thick wooden column. Whispers came from it, soft at first and growing in volume by the second. Cries for help tugged at my heart like a hook sunk in the organ, and tears prickled the back of my eyes.

It didn't want to be here.

I knew it as well as I knew my own name. The book had some sort of consciousness and was begging to be saved from this place. Determination roared inside me, pushing aside all the guilt and dread from what I did tonight. I killed yes, but I would save whatever it was that was keeping this book alive, the plan I had for destroying it long forgotten. The longer I stood and looked at it from across the room, the more certain I was that I was doing the right thing.

"I'll get you out of here," I told it, my voice much stronger than any other time I'd spoken this night. "I'll save you from this evil place."

Somewhere at the back of my mind I was well aware that this was not normal behavior and that something was off. The bodies I left behind haunted my thoughts, preventing any reason or even giving me time to stop and look at it logically. The urge to reach the book was so primal that I wasn't sure I would stop if I had to go through hell itself to get to it. All I knew at the moment was I had to hold it in my arms. Every other reason why I found myself there drifts off like it never existed.

Looking down at myself, I eyed the dirty silk dress that was more black than any other color from the rolling around I did earlier. Taking it off was out of the question since I could only wear panties underneath it because I listened to Glenda and didn't wear a bra. This was what I got for following fashion advise from a seer. Taking hold of the hem, I grabbed two handfuls and ripped it on one side. The silk parted to my hip, the tearing sound making me cringe. Repeating the same thing on the other side, I started folding and twisting it between my legs until I ended up with a horrible-looking silk diaper.

Tia would be screaming for eternity if she ever saw me like this.

A proud grin stretched my lips until it hurt to smile.

"I should've done this sooner."

Chuckling like a mental patient, I reached for my sandals, tugging them off my feet and flinging them away with great satisfaction. When they passed through the magic ropes I froze, the back of my skull tingling from fear that I could be blown to smithereens at any moment. They sailed through the air with no repercussion, thumping loudly when they hit the floor. Blowing out a breath, I smoothed my hair back, twisting it and tying it in a knot. That was one good thing about having long hair, although I doubted it'd stay like that for long.

I scrutinized the magical web spread out in front of me, the whispers and cries of the book egging me on to move faster. The urgency that I had to get to it was like a gun pointed to the back of my head. "Tick tock," it said, "Get to it before they reach this floor." The problem I was facing was a big one, though. I wasn't a contortionist. No matter how I twisted and turned my head to look at it, there was no escaping the fact that I'd have to twist myself like a pretzel to pass some of the entwined ropes. Just to be sure how careful I needed to be, I reached for the closest one, grazing it with the tips of my fingers.

Magic slammed through my palm and pain ricocheted all the way through my shoulder as I dropped my hand limply to my side. Mouth opened in a soundless scream, I swayed on my feet.

"Son of a biscuit ..." Hissing in pain, I blinked fast until the dark spots disappeared from my vision. "No touchy, got it." The words were strained.

So I didn't waste any more time, I cradled my limp arm with the other until the feeling returned to it. Gingerly, I started making my way past the ropes of magic, their glow burning my retinas when my face got too close to them. I didn't dare blink in case I moved slightly and got zapped like a bug. Knowing my penchant for clumsiness kept me alert to the point I crawled too slow over, under, and around them. *It's better be safe than sorry,* I told myself.

A few times my hips or shoulders got too close to the magical web, the crackling of silk and hairs that had escaped the knot making me flinch as my breath got stuck in my throat. Luck might've finally decided that I'd had enough, because before I knew it I was half way through, and the door of the elevator, which disappeared when it closed, chimed open. I froze with one leg in the air and slightly over a rope of magic like a dog about to pee on a fire hydrant. Both my hands—the numb one functioning properly again—were stretched out to my sides to keep my balance, and my chin was held high as if that would help matters somehow.

The Magician stepped onto the floor.

His hate-filled gaze locked on me and his features twisted into a mask of rage. Caught in his stare, I trembled on the spot, my muscles screaming at me from being twisted the way I was. My inner thighs were killing me from holding my body motionless as I watched his eyes dart around the room, probably looking for a way to get to me. The whispers coming from the book sped up, the jumbled-together words urging me to hurry. On the bright side, he was alone. No one else came out before the door closed and left us closed in together.

The Magician

"I see you have more in common with your mother than just your looks." Unbuttoning his tux jacket, he shrugged it off and dropped it at his feet.

"You think?" I panted the question, my limbs trembling and a drop of sweat rolling down the side of my face.

"Cocky, too." His chuckle had no humor in it, the sound of it like ghostly nails scraping the inside of my lobe. "I had other plans for you, Charlie." Sadly shaking his head, his eyes bored into mine like daggers in their intensity. "You proved yourself to be a good asset last night, but you had to go and ruin it all by trying to steal from me."

"Who's stealing?" Blinking innocently at him, I went for a smile, but I could tell it didn't cut it by his narrowed gaze. "I was exercising. Isn't this your training room? I could've sworn that's what I was told."

"Do you even know what you are trying to take?" Ignoring my comment, he removed his cufflinks and unraveled his tie.

"We don't know each other well enough for you to start stripping. You can keep your clothes on." My words fell on deaf ears, and he tugged the loose tie off, letting it drop on top of his jacket.

"It is sad that you have to die." When magic swirled around his fingers, I hopped over the rope because I was desperate to get away from him. "There is nowhere for you to run, girl. Your mother didn't have anywhere to run either." His thin lips curled into a cruel smile that curdled my blood.

Rage erupted in my chest.

"You son of a cracked nut!" I flung magic at him with both hands, searing the skin of my back on the glowing rope behind me.

It hit him in the shoulder, his startled, comical look

telling me he didn't expect it. There would be many things he wasn't expecting that he would experience tonight. Another blast of magic burst out of me, slamming into his chest until his body crashed into the wall behind him, cracking it. I'd never had strong magic like that before, and that was when I noticed the prodding energy at my back. It was tentative and testing, but after that blast it latched onto my skin like a leech.

The magic ropes started pulsing and thickening around me just as The Magician lifted onto his knees. Fury radiated from him in waves, and he sent a torrent of it right for my head. In the panic that came from the fact that he might blow my head open like a watermelon, I forgot about the magical web and stumbled back while ducking to avoid it.

My body passed over the ropes just like the sandals did.

Chapter Seventeen

It was difficult to focus with the whispers from the book buzzing in my ears, the strange energy still poking and prodding at mine, and The Magician flinging magic at me like there was no tomorrow. Passing through the magic web without being fried would've been a blessing if it still didn't hurt like a mother when I did it. Fists clenched tight and shoulders hunched, I spun on my heel and bolted for the thick wooden column that was holding the book. Hurting or not, I had to pass the ropes because it was the only thing I could use as a cover from his assault.

With an enraged scream, he hit me with magic at the center of my back. The hit sent me flying head-first for the column, and I folded my arms around my head to protect my face. Resistance met me like an air bubble around the stand of the book, making me drop like a piece of ripe fruit from a branch in front of it. My hip and shoulder took the brunt of my fall, but somehow I ignored the pain and scrambled around it. Panting, I curled into a ball, shielding my limbs as much as possible. The Magician continued his attack, uncaring that none of his magic hit its target. To my surprise, it also bounced off whatever invisible protection the book had. A relieved breath was wrenched out of my lungs.

Holding my breath, I stuck my head out real fast to see if he had moved any closer. What met my gaze had horror rising in my chest. With his hair sticking out around his head, The Magician was transformed into a thing from my nightmares. His smooth skin and ageless face was ashen, the grayness of the skin tone looking more like stone than flesh. Thin black veins crawled up his neck and fanned over his sunken cheekbones. The whites of his eyes were filled with blood and had so many broken capillaries it was like the entire area around his pale green irises was red. Yellowed, chipped teeth poked from under his snarled, twisted lips.

"It's not time for Halloween yet." I sounded squeaky and a lot like a scared little girl.

"Your parents thought they could keep the Necronomicon from me, too." As spittle flew from his dry cracked lips, he glared at me. "No one is strong enough to withstand its powerful magic but me."

"Have you looked at yourself in the mirror lately?" I shrieked when he threw a flaming ball at me, jerking back behind the column. Ignoring my markings bursting to life and writhing as if they had a mind of their own, I leaned my head back and closed my eyes. "You killed them because you are greedy for power and sick in your head you dumbnut."

A tear made its way down my cheek and over my lips, plopping on my collar bone.

"A guardian, she called herself." A crazed, psychotic laugh came from him, and bile swam in the back of my throat. "Your mother." Like I didn't know who he was referring to. "We saw who was left standing in the end. Me. I'm the only one with enough power to control it."

"It doesn't look like you are controlling anything right now, at least not to me." Rolling my shoulder to alleviate the pain still cramping my muscle, I blew out a breath through pursed lips. "You can't even come closer to it."

If he could pass the wards connecting like a web and protecting the book, he would've been standing over my dead body at the moment. Another ball of magic hit the invisible barrier and bounced off it, but sparks follow in its wake. Craning my neck, I checked to see if it was weakening, but unless it was in contact with something I couldn't even see it. Huddled behind the column as I was gave me a minute to breathe, and now that I had the energy, it was time to see if I could reach the book. Turning to face it on my knees, I bit my lips hard and tentatively reached out with my hand.

Resistance met my touch for long enough I almost pulled my hand away. The energy prodding at mine intensified and my hand passed through the protection, which forced me to lean heavily forward. The moment my chest was pressed hard on the wooden column all the whispers crowding my mind stopped, leaving a ringing sound in my ears.

My palm landed on the cool, aged cover of the book.

Something powerful and old woke up and reached for me from deep within my soul. The magic I felt before was ancient, but this was something older than time itself. Horror choked me, but I couldn't move to pull my hand away from the book. It whispered sweet promises in my head, offering me an eternal life of power and glory if I only allowed it to join me. It wanted to come to my world and share it with me.

I wanted that, too.

I wanted it so bad it hurt inside. It was the friend I never had. Something that would be by my side through thick and thin and help me get revenge for my parents. It would destroy everyone that had ever wronged me, and it would make me the most feared being alive. I really wanted to be feared. All I had to do was open the book and feed it my blood. I could do that. No one could stop me. The voice kept whispering nothings in my mind, while my fingers inched closer to the edge of the book. It told me how powerful I was, that together we would make this world as it should be.

The Magician roared his rage from a distance, but it was insignificant.

The old being told me the monster was nothing. If I let it out it would destroy him. It would kill him along with Master Bowmen, Jonas, and everyone else. Nigel would pay for his duplicity, as well. Gray eyes full of something I couldn't name float in front of my mind's eye, silencing the voice. The vampire's cocky smirk playing on his lips made me blink, which pulled me out of the fog that was clouding my head. With a jerk I yanked my hand away from the book, gasping for air.

"Fiddlesticks." Breathing the word, I crabwalked away from the column, completely horrified by what I almost did.

"You will die and I will feed on your magic," the Magician snarled, his voice finally coming out loud, clear, and much closer than before.

A faint chime rang from the elevator door.

"Ms. Jansen." Nigel's deep voice snapped like a whip in the air. "Ms. Jansen." Leave it to the vampire to stick to propriety at a time like this.

"Blade, we need to get rid of the girl." The Magician

growled, and I changed direction to crawl forward and warn the vampire. "If you want the power I promised you, you'll help."

"Where is she?" Sticking my head out, I saw Nigel staring daggers at The Magician, his fangs poking from under his upper lip. Understanding dawned on the monster's face and his lip quivered in rage.

"Watch out." My shout was too late.

Magic sent Nigel crashing in the wall, his head snapping back and hitting it with a sickening crunch. The Magician laughed like a psycho as he turned those creepy eyes on me. Insanity lurked in them, making my lungs squeeze painfully. I doubted the vampire survived that much magic. We could withstand it because it was part of our makeup. It was what we were, and we were nothing without it. Other factions could never withstand half of what that son of a crackednut used on Nigel. As much as I disliked the dimwit, I wasn't sure I wanted him dead.

Tears prickled the back of my eyes.

Lifting on my feet, I flung my wrists to the side and released my swords. This monster had killed enough people and had to be stopped. For my parents, for Nigel, and for all the others that I didn't know the names of. Preserving life had always been my dream. But he was not life. This warped creature in front of me was a virus, a disease that needed to be cured. Removed.

The Magician faced me with triumph plastered on his face, his eyes eerily glinting in his madness. I had the opportunity to see firsthand what greed and too much power did to a person. The magic he tried to hit me with bounced off my sword when I blocked it. His eyes widened and he snarled at me like a rabid beast.

"This is the night you die," I told him, not recognizing my own voice.

"And who's going to kill me?" Laughing hysterically, he moved closer. "You, little girl? I have the Necronomicon under my control. Nothing can kill me."

Doubt tried to crawl inside me but I shoved it away. I had to kill him. Anything else was unacceptable. Another fiery ball sailed my way and I blocked it again. Bouncing on the balls of my feet, I sprinted at him and slashed both swords at his neck. Jerking back, he avoided the killing blow and hit me with the heel of his palm in the sternum. Grunting in pain, I danced away from him, spinning in a circle and slicing one of the swords in an arch at his chest. The sizzling of seared flesh and the stench of burned meat made me smile. His scream was music to my ears.

We circled each other, lashing out and flinging magic, I ground my teeth every time I walked through a magical rope, and he ducked under and jumped over them when he noticed them near him. When they skipped his notice, his flesh sizzled like a roast, saturating the air with a horrendous odor. My markings kept writhing, The Magician burned my skin with his magic faster than they could heal it. Pure stubbornness and hatred for the monster kept me fighting and on my feet.

"You should be looking out for all of us, not killing us off for your own greed." Pushing the words through clenched teeth, I stabbed at his stomach, but he spun away from the attack.

"Soon enough you'll join them, and I'll be that much stronger after taking your power." Stopping in his tracks, he started muttering under his breath.

At first I thought he'd finally snapped, that the insanity had taken over his mind. Then dread turned my blood to

The Magician

ice when I realized what he was doing. The son of a biscuit was chanting spells. Sorcery had been forbidden for centuries. We were only allowed to use our own magic, and for a very good reason. Back in the old days, spells would bind the powers of others or steal it for whoever was using them. All spell books had been burned and everyone that used sorcery killed. No one today should know how to perform it.

Apparently, The Magician didn't get the memo.

A large circle came to life at his chanting, spinning around the book. Panic gripped me when sigils popped inside it, pulsing like a heartbeat and getting brighter the longer he spoke. Eyes closed, he didn't care that I was standing close enough that all I had to do was jump forward and stab him with my swords. Was it a trap? Was he trying to fool me into thinking it was easy just so he could pull a new trick out of thin air? Unwilling to leave it to chance, trap or not, I pulled both elbows back and bounced off the balls of my feet, sinking both swords in the center of his chest. We were so close our noses almost touched.

His eyes snapped open, the shock in them unmistakable.

"It cannot be." Blood sprayed my face from his lips with each word.

"This is for my parents." Twisting both swords slowly, I watched every pained twitch of the muscles on his face. "Die."

His nails shredded the skin on my arms, a last-ditch effort of a dying beast to inflict pain on another. I didn't look away from his wide eyes until the life in them blinked out and only the empty shell of the monster was left behind. I waited for a while though, just in case he was faking it, but the weight of his body became too much. Stepping away, I allowed him to slide off my swords before I uncurled my fingers, dropping them. Lifting my head, I watched the glowing circle around the book. The light was dimming, but it didn't look like it was going away.

Gingerly, I stepped closer, and not knowing what else to do, I reached my fingers to touch the book. The energy was still prodding but not as strong as before. When my fingers were just a hairsbreadth away from it, the book flipped open and I jumped back with a strangled scream. The pages turned fast as if there was an invisible wind moving them, then all movement stopped as the book settled on one—a picture of a wizard.

A thick cloud of smoke billowed out, spilling over the pages and down the wooden column. It crawled like a snake to the dead carcass of The Magician until it covered him completely. Writhing over him, the sucking, slurping noises made me sick and I gagged, inching around it. Before I knew it, it started slinking back, disappearing up the column and inside the book. The book fluttered again, spitting out a card before slamming shut.

My eyes darting from the card on the floor lying face down to the book, I warily got closer and reached to pick it up. When I turned it to see which one it was, I sucked in a sharp breath. It was a tarot card. And as scary as it might be, my gaze fell to the floor where the body of the monster used to be. There was nothing there now. My eyes snapped back to the card.

The Magician.

Turning my head slowly to the side, I stared at the book. The thought of destroying it made my knees wobble and bile rise in my throat. Without trying, I knew I wouldn't be able to burn it, even if the circle was not still pulsing around it. At least the monster was dead. I'd find a place to hide the book where no one would find it. I had to. Sticking the card in my boobs, I wrinkled my nose. With a weary sigh, I scrubbed a hand over my face, wincing at all the scrapes and bruises I had all over me from the fight. My tongue poked out, prodding at my split lip where he got me with an elbow. It'd heal, I just didn't have the energy to heal myself right now.

Not knowing what else to do, I flung some small magic at the glowing sigils around the book, although I was standing too close to it. It sent a strong spark once forcing me to flinch, and the whole circle blinked out. Excitement bubbled inside me, and grinning like a fool, I whooped while punching my fist in the air.

Bad idea.

My arm hit the wooden column and it wobbled harshly. The book rattled before it started sliding off when it pitched forward. A breath lodged in my throat, I flung my hands forward to catch it before it hit the floor. Fear of the sucking shadow was the only thought in my mind. The books slid off the column, opening as it dropped on my blood covered hands. Glenda's words sounded loud and clear in my head like a curse. *"No matter what the situation Charlie, don't open the book."*

A dark chuckle echoed around me.

"Mother fudging fiddlesticks!" I hissed.

Darkness took me away.

Chapter Eighteen

"You think she used glue or something?" a familiar female's voice penetrated the church bells in my head as someone tugged on my arm.

"Why in the world would she use glue?" I knew this second voice. It was Glenda. "She has magic."

"Excuseeee me, how could the poor human forget that you guys have magic. You rub it in my face every day," the first one sneered.

"You just found out about us," Glenda deadpanned.

Finally, I remembered the first one. Tia. A jolt of panic stabbed me in the chest and my eyes popped open. Bright lights burned my retinas. I closed them with a groan curling up around myself. The bickering stopped and cool hands touched my arms as they turned me around.

"Charlie?" Tia sounded excited, and the next thing I knew she was slapping me on the face. "Charlie, are you alive?"

"You won't be if you keep hitting me." I tried to smack her hands away, but something weighed my arm down.

Keeping my eyelids lifted to slits, I tried to see how they managed to come to the cursed floor. Even better, how did the two of them reach me past the magical ropes crisscrossing the space. When I saw the wide room where the ball was had, the tables still sprinkled around, my body jerked and I almost headbutted Tia.

"How did you bring me here?" I looked between them, noticing the confusion at the question.

"You came down yourself." Tia ducked her head and stared at me like I was crazy. "I was looking for you when you stumbled out of a door. I couldn't find it after that. Weird really." Her eyes widened for emphasis.

"Nig—" Cutting myself off from using his real name, I coughed to cover the slip up. Glenda give me a knowing look that I ignored. "Blade? Have you seen him?"

"Who?" Tia wrinkled her nose at me.

"You were dragging him with you. He was unconscious," Glenda said, avoiding my gaze. "A girl came with silver hair. Mean one, too." Frowning at the ground, she balled her fists. "I tried to stop her, but she snapped at me and took him away saying he was her responsibility. She even tried to take you with her, but you said something in a foreign language and she blanched before taking a step away from you. I was going to block her from leaving, but she had an elder wood wand." Shivering, she finally met my eyes.

"Selina." Remembering the witch, I couldn't say I blamed Glenda. I stood frozen too thanks to her. The scary part was that I didn't remember anything after catching the book from falling. "But he was alive?" Too afraid to hope, I slapped Tia's hands when she tugged on my twisted dress, which had turned into shorts.

"He was breathing if that's what you're asking."

"Yeah, your friend here had no trouble feeling him up to check for a pulse," Tia chirped, grinning at Glenda's bright red face.

Shaking my head, I finally saw why I couldn't slap Tia's hands. The book was cradled in my hand like it belonged there. My heart stopped for a long beat before jackhammering my chest. Everything that happened returned to me and dread numbed me. When I tried to drop it, it didn't move an inch. Luckily there was no one else there but the three of us.

"Want to share why you look like you were fighting with wolves while dressed like an adult toddler from a fetish porn movie?" Tia cocked an eyebrow while looking at my dress with disgust.

"Sorry, I didn't pay attention to the dress code while trying to stay alive." Annoyed, I pushed to my feet. "Where is everyone?"

"They are looking for The Magician." Glenda scrambled to her feet as well. "When his wards around the guild dropped, it was mass hysteria down here. Master Bowmen had to take control of the guild."

"My uncle is in charge of the guild now?" I guessed it could be worse, but he did have some greed in him, and I could see it turning him into the same monster I killed upstairs.

"I can't believe I'm included in all this." Tia breathed, vibrating from happiness. At my sharp look, she pouted. "What? It's exciting, yo! Which human can say they hang around mages and ..." Squinting at Glenda, she pursed her lips. "What were you again?"

"Seer." Glenda fidgeted, her face brightening with red blotches across her cheekbones, and my gut clenched for her.

"She can see things before they happen. It's an amazing gift and greatly revered." At Glenda's startled gaze, I smiled at her. She did warn me about what could happen after all. It was my fault I didn't do what she told me to.

"We should go home." Glancing nervously around, I couldn't wait to get out of there before someone saw the book. "We can't let anyone know about this." Waving the book between us, I made sure both of them understood the importance.

"You can't go back to the clan." Glenda latched onto my forearm, staying as far away from the old book as possible. "That much I can say. If you do go back, many will die. Including you."

"Where the hell will I go if not home?"

"My place," Tia jumped in eagerly. "Don't look at me like that, Charlie. If you have a better idea, I'm all ears. And yes, I'm a sidekick so I'm going where you are going."

After a groan, I closed my eyes and took a deep breath. Tia would be the death of me. No Magician or old ancient evil had anything on the human. The sad part was, she knew it, too.

"I'll come too," Glenda chirped. "I can be useful." There was so much hope in her voice I decided what the hell. If we were going down, we would do it together.

Strangely, warmth spread through my chest at the thought.

"Okay, let's move before anyone sees us," I urged them both.

"This way." Tia spun on her heel and bolted across the wide room. "We can use the staff entrance so no one will see us leaving."

"And you know this how?" the human is a pain in the butt, but a useful one.

"It's how I snuck in" ginning over her shoulder she didn't slow down.

Glenda and I glanced at each other and followed after the blonde terror. She was the least dangerous yet the most vicious of us all. The book slipped from my hand, hitting the floor with a resounding thump. We all froze, Tia jumping around to stare at us in horror. Wind blasted through the room, ruffling the pages when the book opened, and disappearing when it stopped on a different type of drawing on it. I dreaded looking at it, but I couldn't help myself.

A woman was perched on a throne with a new moon shining above her head. Two fingers were lifted pointing up on one hand and she held a crystal ball in the other. A mysterious, knowing smile was slightly curving up the corners of her lips.

I frowned at it.

Reaching in the top of my dress, I pulled out the card and stared from it to the page of the open book. I'd never been interested in tarot, and I regretted that fact now. I had no idea what I was looking at. Glenda took my wrist gingerly, turning the card to her. The only sign that she was freaked out was the increased speed of her breathing.

"The Magician." The word was a breath passing her lips.

"What is it?" When her eyes snapped to mine, I jutted my chin and pointed at the book. "Which one is that?" She glanced down at it, her fingers tightening on my wrist.

"The High Priestess." Swallowing thickly, she kept staring at it.

Selina waving that damn wand came to mind, and lead pooled in my stomach. Let's hope it wasn't her that would rear an evil head. I dealt with The Magician, so I would deal with her too if I had to. I really hoped I didn't have to.

"What does it mean?" Tia peeked down at the open book, too.

Swiping it up, I snapped it shut and tucked it under my arm. "Nothing. Let's hide the book and get some rest first. We can think of our next move tomorrow."

We all trickled out of the guild into the night, the cold breeze doing nothing to cool my skin. With one last look over my shoulder at the tall building, I followed the two women to Tia's place. I'd go looking for Nigel tomorrow and make sure he was okay. He was a self-centered son of a biscuit and as arrogant as they came, but at the end, I got the feeling he wasn't as evil as the rest of them. It was just something about him that I couldn't really hate him even when I wanted to. There was more to the vampire than met the eye. Tonight, everything was as it should be. The bad was behind me, right? How much worse could things get?

I should've known better than to say those famous last words.

Next in The Necronomicon Guardian series

vinci-books.com/thehighpriestess

Power has a price—and she's paying.

Charlie never planned on controlling the most evil creatures in existence. But after accidentally opening the Gate of the Gods, she's bound to the Necronomicon. With dark forces closing in, even her fiercest ally may be her greatest threat.

Turn the page for a free preview…

The High Priestess: Prologue

It had been a week since my life took a turn for the worse, sending me in a downward spiral that would lead me on a path with no positive outcome at the end. Struggling with my powers and making sure I stayed alive in a house full of killers seemed like a walk in the park compared to being bonded to a book the supernatural world would kill to get their hands on. As you know by now, I was the unfortunate soul who got shackled to it the night I killed the one person I hated with the strength of a hundred burning suns. The slug killed my parents, so I killed him in return. Unfortunately Karma smacked me in the face and dealt me a new set of cards.

The Magician was gone, his body turning into a tarot card I kept because of a nagging feeling I might need it in the future. The bloodsucker who forced me to go and steal from the leader of the mage faction almost died himself in the fight, which left me confused as hell about why he even bothered coming to my aid in the first place. Making sure that the book ended up in his hands could've been what brought him barging in the room, but that still didn't explain why he was threating The Magician in an attempt to protect me.

Nothing made sense.

Coming to Tia's apartment and dragging Glenda with me might've been a bad idea too, but neither her nor I could go back home. My uncle took control of the Mage's guild, holding the position of the Magician, and with that making sure I couldn't go anywhere near him. If I did, he would know I was trying to hide something. I had never been good at lying, and without Tia's help there was no way I would've pulled off the biggest lie I'd ever told: Nigel Thatcher was dead. The fact that the bloodsucker was prancing under their noses and going by the name of Blade was a whole new bullcrap I didn't have energy left to decipher.

Tia and Glenda spent two days interrogating me about what had actually happened and what it all meant for us until I was so frustrated that I told them everything just so I could have a moment of peace. Now I couldn't step foot outside without them following me like a bad smell and calling themselves my sidekicks. I knew it was all Tia's fault, but there was nothing I could do about it. The picture of the High Priestess the Necronomicon showed me that my troubles were just beginning, and if I wanted to survive, I needed to make sure Nigel Thatcher was alive. He had more information about the Necronomicon than any other person I knew, and I needed to corner him to find out just how deep the rabbit hole went.

Speaking of rabbits, the glass statues of the long-eared buggers sprinkled around the hotel Nigel was using seemed very fitting. It was my next stop, if only I could find a way to escape the two women adamant on coming with me. It should be easy for an assassin to sneak out.

A normal assassin could pull it off for sure.

A clumsy one like me? Not so much.

Still, I had to try.

Wish me luck.

The High Priestess: Chapter One

Granby street was buzzing with activity as I sulked in the shadows behind the same tree I used as cover in hopes of finding any information on Nigel Thatcher. That was the time in the past when I was naïve and I thought I had any chance of assassinating the elusive vampire. I totally expected that son of a cracked nut to give me an ulcer by the time I killed him. I didn't end up with that diagnosis, but I did get shackled to a more sinister pain in my tush. The whispers slithering through my mind sounded distant the further I was from the damn Necronomicon book, but they were there. A constant inside me, reminding me that my life has gone to neverland, and no wishing or yelping "oweee" would make it go away.

No, I was royally fudged.

The IRS parking lot was almost empty—as per usual at the time of the night—only tonight it was giving me unnecessary anxiety. I couldn't understand the reason, but I knew deep down that something was going to happen. Rubbing my sweaty palms off the fabric on my pants, I stared up at the puffs of gray clouds stretching like a beaded necklace above the Glass Light Hotel and Gallery. As I watched, they floated through the dark sky to hide the few stars sprinkled through it. I had an inkling that this was where Selena took Nigel, and I had every intention on talking to the bloodsucker tonight.

It was his fault I was in this mess.

My heart hammering against my ribs, I locked my gaze on the hotel's front doors and glared at them like all of this was somehow their doing. The rustling behind me stiffened my spine and I braced as if I was about to be attacked. But it wasn't an attacker. I'd recognize the energy slamming into my back anywhere, even if my eyes were closed.

"Let me tell you how the story goes." The whispered words were enthusiastic enough to make me grind my teeth. "This is a rollercoaster of a ride—"

"Tia, if you don't stop it, I swear I will zap you. Why are you here?" Hissing at her over my shoulder, I clenched my fists so I didn't grab her by the neck when she grinned at me like a fool.

"What do you mean, 'why am I here?'" Undeterred, she rushed to my side, her eyes wide with excitement. "Sidekick, hello! Where you go, I go. All the adventures of the hero need to be recorded by yours truly. You're welcome, by the way. I won't charge a penny for anything."

"I'm not sure she appreciates humor, or us being here," Glenda muttered under her breath, edging nearer while tugging on Tia's shirt to prevent her from coming closer to me. The seer knew me well enough to know not to get within arm's reach of me when I was angry. "I told you it was a bad idea."

"Yeah. She needs to work on her gratitude issues."

Somehow Tia managed to take their interference and turn it around to make me the bad guy in the situation.

The giddy twinkle in their eyes and the eagerness plastered all over their faces did not match the apologetic words they murmured as they crowded around me, but their nearness did give me a case of claustrophobia. To my horror, I also realized both were dressed in all black, their pants and long-sleeved shirts sticking tight to their bodies and paired with soft-soled boots to hide their footsteps. My gaze snapped from their feet to Glenda's face and she had the decency to look ashamed.

"I had to sneak back in the clan manor and get some of my things." The seer told the tips of her boots, her pale face darkening at her cheekbones. "You left, and to stop Tia from following you, I asked her to come with me. Not that it worked, but yeah. She waited, hidden across the street." Glenda rushed to assure me when I sucked in a sharp breath. "I figured no one would care that a few pair of boots went missing. What, with everything going on, they could've gotten misplaced ... or something."

"I must've done something horrible in my past lives to be punished like this." Groaning, I turned my back on both of them and rubbed a hand harshly over my face in frustration. "This is Karma in the works right here." Taking a deep breath and blowing it out slowly, I scanned the front of the hotel across the street, seeing nothing. "At least you blend in with the shadows and no one will see you here, since this is where you will stay so I don't kill you both. There is that."

"Oh, look." Whisper-yelling, Tia ignored my threat and yanked on my arm to make me look at what she was trying to show me. "I made sure we have our signature added to the outfits, too." Puffing out her chest, she pointed a finger at her left boob.

I blinked stupidly, not understanding.

This night was going to smithereens really fast and I'd only been stalking the hotel for a couple of hours. My friends were adding to the disaster, and not just because they followed me here, but also because they were talking in riddles, which was making a heartbeat pound in my temples. The confusion I felt was obvious to both women, who held their breath while they waited on my reaction. Tia looked down and her eyes widened as if something clicked, then she stepped out of the thick shadow cast by the tree until the yellow glow of the streetlight fell on her chest. My stomach dropped and the base of my skull went numb when I finally saw what she'd been trying to reveal. Right there, on top of her left boob in elaborate swirls, were my clan's emblem, two dragons twining together, and my initials. Darting my gaze to Glenda's chest, I saw it on her shirt, as well.

A jolt of magic coursed through me until my fingers twitched and tingled.

Fear ... shock ... I had no idea what it was, but it was trying to strangle me.

"I made it the exact shade of blue." Oblivious to my turmoil while I wrestled with my magic and did everything possible for my swords not to appear in my hands, Tia kept jabbering on. "It matches the color of your eyes," she informed me proudly, while Glenda nodded in encouragement from behind her. They had a death wish, both of them. "When you do your thing, only your eyes can be seen with that face covering you wear. It's a perfect signature, I'm telling you."

"Umm, Tia?" The timid way Glenda's voice filled the silence matched the way she inched away from me when her eyes zeroed in on my fingers, which were spasming as I fought the urge to release my power. Of course, the human ignored all signs of danger. Typical Tia, if you knew the girl. "I think we should go ... like now."

"Don't be absurd." Jerking her arm out of Glenda's grip, Tia stepped closer to me and a grin stretched her face. I realized in disbelief that she had makeup on, and a tiny dragon painted with eyeliner on the top of her cheekbone. It looked like a beauty mark when she was further away from me, but now it was mocking me. And all I could do was gape at it.

My mouth worked soundlessly.

"Sooo, are we going in to get intel or what? We can spread out, that way we can do it faster. It's what they do in all the spy movies I've watched ... I think." Tia muttered the last part under her breath, though her words still sent my eyebrows to my hairline. "I could get a nun to confess her sins if I put my mind to it. We will find the hottie in no time ... well, as long as I corner one of the hotel workers." Latching onto my forearm, she shook me in her excitement. "What do you think I should go for? Bad cop or good cop? I think bad cop will work the best, especially if they hear you swear. No way you can pull off bad cop. No offense Charlie."

I could hear her voice coming from far away, the sound echoing as if it was coming from underwater. A red haze blanketed my vision, one specific remark throbbing in repeat through my head. *"She'll find the hottie."* My internal voice mocked me, even adding sinister chuckles to drive the point home. The light coming from the street reflected off the glittery substance Tia used to draw the dragons and my initials on her shirt. Another joke on my account, and it laughed at me in the face. Somewhere deep down I was aware this behavior was unlike me and had everything to do with my connection to the cursed book, but I was too gone to stop what was about to happen. My rational brain screamed in panic because my friend was standing too close to me. Unfortunately, I was beyond the point of no return.

Everything happened too fast to track.

My fingers snapped open and stretched wide. The weight and the cool feel of metal instantly settled in my palms when both swords shot out. On their own, my arms moved, the muscle memory guiding my actions and slashing the air in an upward arch. My heart stopped when a flash of red passed in a blur before my eyes, and Tia's yelp followed right behind it. That was Tia's blood spraying from a wound I had caused, and I knew it from the bottom of my heart.

The horror didn't end there. My other hand cocked in preparation to remove the object of my anger at all costs. No struggling could gain me the control I so desperately wanted. Grunts and groans bounced off the pavement, the noises finally snapping me out of my daze in time to change the trajectory of my sword. I wished the returning logic had flicked my hand outward, but it didn't. No, it twisted the blade inward and the sword glided into my own thigh like it was slipping through butter. My mouth snapped shut, and my teeth clenched so hard I thought I broke a molar.

"The fuck is the matter with you?" Tia's anger was a tangible thing curling around my ears, and the best sound I had heard in my life.

I didn't kill her.

My knees buckled more from that knowledge than the excruciating pain in my leg. Blinking fast to clear my vision, I looked down to find them both—her and Glenda—sprawled on the ground at my feet. Two pairs of glaring eyes were focused on my face, but I couldn't care less. A blur of red tackled Tia away from my weapon, and I realized soon after seeing it that it was Glenda's hair. If I wasn't so happy none of them were hurt I would've wondered how she managed to be so fast. That thought evaporated when another wave of searing pain passed through the muscle of my thigh, which reminded me I still had a magical sword sticking from it.

"Oh my God, you stabbed yourself." Tia, ever the observant, forgot about her anger as she scrambled on the ground and lifted to her knees, blinking in amazement at my bleeding leg. "Who does that?"

Embarrassment hit me out of nowhere, that question bringing old insecurities about being an Assassin Mage to the forefront of my mind. A lump formed in my throat. Attempting to play it off as nothing more than a scratch, I grinded my teeth to stop myself from crying out in pain when I reached for the trunk of the tree to lean on it.

"It's nothing." A squeak ripped from my throat when my hand missed the tree and I went toppling to the side.

My gaze locked on Glenda's, her owlish stare adding to my spiked heartrate a second before I hit the ground. The sword jostled in my leg and sent a fresh wave of agony through me, which only added to the pain from the impact my whole left side took when it kissed the unforgiving concrete. My head bouncing off the pavement, I rolled on my back and waited for the burst of stars behind my eyelids to go away. When my vision cleared and the agony had subsided, I didn't want to open my eyes. I could feel the heat from the bodies on both sides of me. When they didn't go away after a few minutes, an oppressive silence tugged on my neck like an anvil until I blinked. I had no choice then, so I focused on the two faces leaning over my head.

"Oweeee."

My whisper-yell made Glenda's lips twitch at the corners, though she flinched while at the same time. At least I thought it was because of that, but then Tia yanked the sword from my leg and I bit my tongue so hard I tasted blood.

"There." The clinking of metal bouncing off the ground faded with the rushing of blood in my ears. "She should heal on her own now, right? I didn't just kill her?" Tia's eyes were on Glenda for confirmation, while I debated on taking the sword and this time really stabbing her in the eye.

"Yeah." The seer nodded, her eyes never leaving me. It was almost as if she was reading my mind and expecting me to do what I was thinking. "She'll heal, but I'd stay away from her if I were you, at least for a while."

"Whatever. This is why she needs a side kick. I'm hoping bleeding in a parking lot will bring that point home." Tia huffed, and I turned to her because I was astonished that she really didn't give a damn about her life. "It's Charlie. She wouldn't hurt a fly, little less me. Have you met the girl?" When Glenda's gaping expression matched my own, the human chuckled. "Now ... when are we getting inside the hotel?"

"It's going to be a long night." I groaned as I stared at the sky and rethought my life choices, though it was difficult not to scream as my skin knitted back together and wave after excruciating wave of never ending pain crashed through me.

"Yup," Glenda chirped, and then she stiffened and peered over her shoulder at the entrance of the hotel, adding to my misery with her next words. "And if that's who I think it is, things just got much, much more interesting."

The High Priestess: Chapter Two

"What is that dimwit doing here?" Wincing from the tightness of my freshly healed skin when I lifted on my knees, I glared at the person exiting a black vehicle parked at the front of the hotel.

"Who are we talking about?" Tia wiggled between Glenda and me, squinting to see what we were looking at.

"Jonas," Glenda spat the name in disgust, reflecting my sentiment when it came to that particular mage.

"The first target was spotted and is about to be eliminated," Tia whispered in a rush as she bent her head to her chest.

Reluctantly pulling my gaze from Jonas just as he disappeared through the front doors into the belly of the hotel, I incredulously turned it on my friend. "What are you doing?"

"Nothing." Her head jerked up and she shoved her left hand behind her back. Glenda's pained groan did not help matters either.

"Tia."

The Magician

Hissing her name as a warning, I stared her down until she huffed a breath and dropped her shoulders in defeat. Sluggishly she brought her arm around in front of her and uncurled her fingers from a black device that resembled a remote control. No, not a remote control.

A mother-trucking recording device.

"Hey!" she yelped when I snatched it from her hand and clawed at the air in a futile attempt to get it back.

Holding it away from her, I battled with my frustration while sending a wave of magic through my hand into the device to destroy it. Better it than zapping my friend for this stupidity. Sparks burst from it, frying it and blistering my own skin in the process. My teeth clenched, and I swallowed the scream that tried to push through my lips. Just because I ended up bound to the Necronomicon didn't mean I had miraculously gained control over my powers. They still worked more against me than for me, as demonstrated with the recorder.

"The two of you need to go home, now." Sounding pained—because I was in pain with my newly blistered palm—I shook my hand to drop the now melted plastic. "I can't do this if I have to worry about you, too."

"I just didn't want to forget any details," Tia grumbled, pouting like a petulant child while looking at the lump of plastic next to my leg. "You didn't have to destroy it. All you had to do was tell me to put it away."

I stared at her.

"Come on." Glenda, never the one to handle drama well, tugged on Tia's arm. "Let's go guard the book while she does her thing. She will tell us when she needs our help." Giving me a pointed look, the seer jumped to her feet. "Right, Charlie?"

After a long stare down I said what was expected. "Right."

Anxiety was eating a hole in my stomach. I wanted to barge inside the hotel and find Nigel. Also, I desperately wanted to know what Jonas was doing here. And I needed these two brickheads to go home where they would be safe. My thoughts must've been clear on my face because Tia didn't argue, although she glared at me while Glenda dragged her away. I waited until they disappeared into the darkness of the parking lot before bringing my hand to my chest and cradling it.

"Oweee." I blew on the blisters, although I knew it won't help. And as I expected it didn't do much, not until they start healing anyway.

The wind whistled through the branches swaying above my head, the occasional horn and roaring of vehicles accompanying it in a distant melody penetrating the rushing of blood in my ears. Melted plastic smarted like the dickens on bare skin, but I'd go to my grave before I admitted it to anyone. Left alone with no witnesses, I permitted one tear to trickle down my cheek before squaring my shoulders and getting my head in the game.

Opening my hand, I called back the sword I'd dropped earlier when I almost mutilated myself, feeling the weapons blend into my skin. *You got this, Charlie*, I told myself a few times while scanning the street. My eyes lifted up the tall building and past the few spotlights shooting sheets of yellow light skyward, until they stopped at a familiar window on the fifth floor.

My heart skipped a beat when the curtains that were pulled tightly over it shifted as if someone was peeking through them. With my heartbeat in my throat, I watched it unblinking, not daring to even breathe. Though when dark spots danced in front of my eyes I had no choice. Did that son of a cracked nut know I was here? If he did, would there be another trap waiting for me as soon as I dared step foot inside?

At this point, I was tapped-out and bone weary from everything, and the picture of the high priestess the night the book opened danced in front of my mind's eye. Every time I thought of that I remembered Selena perched on the window twirling the elder wood wand. It didn't make sense that she would be in the same bucket as the Magician, did it? She was helping Nigel get the book, wasn't she?

Nothing made sense.

All this was making me dizzy.

The pain in my hand was mostly gone, so I blew out a breath, shaking my palm as if I was trying to get rid of cobwebs that were stuck to it. My wrist cracked, the sound too loud to my ears in the sudden silence that blanketed the air around me. Freezing, I strained to hear the rustling of the leaves or the soft murmuring of the wind through the branches, but I was met with no luck. As if someone has pressed mute, the space around me continued the motions but nothing made a peep.

A tingling feeling started at my fingertips, and my heart raced, flipflopping wildly in my chest so hard my ribs hurt from it. Cold sweat trickled down my spine when numbness spread from my shoulders up the back of my neck, settling at the base of my skull. An invisible force pulled my gaze to the front entrance of the hotel, and my lips parted when two people walked out.

Jonas exited first, his head swiveling left and right as his dark, beady eyes scanned the street. After his perusal was complete, he moved to the side to hold the door open for the person behind him. Dressed in a smart suit with her hair tightly coiled in a bun at the base of her head, Selina stepped out with her shoulders back and her face an unreadable mask. She walked as if she was doing the cemented ground a favor by gracing it with her feet. I shrunk back further in the shadows, half hiding myself behind the trunk of the tree, and half praying that they wouldn't notice they were being watched. A million questions bombarded my brain, but none stayed long enough for me to grasp.

I watched as they stepped to the curb, and the black car glided smoothly in front of them. The back door opened while the vehicle was still moving, and Selena was already sliding inside it. As her head ducked in, I was about to move, but instead my fingers dug into the bark of the tree when Jonas's gaze snapped in my direction. *Please, look away. Please, look away...* my mind screamed. I might hate the mother trucker, but I wasn't ready to deal with him yet. The whispers that were constant in the back of my mind connecting me to the book intensified, humming insistently and bouncing through my panicked brain.

His eyebrows dipped low over his eyes, a line slicing between them while he blinked a few times and shook his head. My heart stopped when the hand he had pressed on the open door dropped to his side, but Jonas didn't come to investigate. With one last confused look my way, he followed Selena and disappeared inside the idling car. The vehicle peeled off the sidewalk flowing into the traffic until the back red lights blinked to life like demon's eyes when it stopped at the corner before taking a right.

I jumped a foot off the ground and twisted an ankle when the sound returned with a loud snap like a popping balloon. All the fudge in the world couldn't help while I jumped in a circle on one foot and gripped my sore ankle as if I was performing a tribal dance and calling the rain. Just a bonfire was missing to add to my embarrassment. Soft snickering came from behind me, but when I whirled around there was no one there.

"Great, Charlie. You are not just a clumsy dimwit, you're hearing things, too." Muttering under my breath, I pressed a thumb and a forefinger to the bridge of my nose, pressing hard enough for colors to burst behind my closed eyelids. "Which gods have I angered this time to be punished like this?"

Grab your copy...
vinci-books.com/thehighpriestess

About the Author

Maya Daniels, USA Today Bestselling and multi-award-winning supernatural suspense author, is a fun-loving woman with many talents.

She traveled the world, gaining life experiences that helped her career as an investigative journalist, as well as her storytelling. Maya writes compelling tales of magic, mythical creatures, loyalty, and life-changing friendships with snarky female characters—much like herself.

Her travels have taken her to Europe, Africa, Asia, Australia, and America. Born with her feet in motion, she currently resides in Ohio, spinning her next epic story that you will not want to put down.

Her biggest 'sins' are her love of chocolate and coffee—through an IV drip! One to never sit still, Maya practices Reiki healing, different types of martial arts, reads about the arcane, talks to furry creatures more than humans, picks up a sledgehammer for home improvement, and travels with her fated mate, seeking her own adventures.